"You told me that you have two strikes against you if push comes to shove over custody of the boys. The first was your past."

He nodded slowly, unsure where she was going with this.

"But you've never been arrested and most of the stories of your legendary antics were in the tabloids, right?" she continued.

"Right," he agreed. "Those tabloid reports were always full of untruths and exaggerations."

"You've kept a very low profile since moving back here to the ranch, and nobody can make a case that you aren't an upstanding citizen now."

He quirked a brow. "Go on…"

"So really the only issue is the fact that you're a single man trying to raise two children alone. We could fix that." She took a deep breath. "We would make sure that their grandfather couldn't use that fact against you."

"And how would we do that?" he asked.

She held his gaze intently. "You could marry me."

Dear Reader,

Do you believe in love at first sight? Did you see your mate across a crowded room and feel that inexplicable crazy tingle, the magic of an immediate connection? According to recent studies, forty-eight percent of men and forty-nine percent of women believe in the phenomenon of love at first sight.

That's the way love happened for me. I saw my husband and in that first sight, before I had exchanged a single word with him, I knew he was a man I could love.

For my heroine in this book, love comes quickly for former bad boy Jack, but the most difficult part of love at first sight is figuring out if it's a simple case of lust or something more meaningful that will withstand the test of time.

Love at first sight is a terrific beginning for a relationship, but it takes time and shared experiences, laughter and perhaps a few tears to discern the true depth of that love.

I had love at first sight, but I'm hoping when the ride is over and I'm old and gray, that I'll have love at last sight as well.

Best,

Carla Cassidy

CARLA CASSIDY

5 Minutes to Marriage

Silhouette

Romantic

SUSPENSE

Special thanks and acknowledgment to Carla Cassidy for
her contribution to the Love in 60 Seconds miniseries.

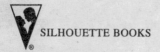

SILHOUETTE BOOKS

Recycling programs
for this product may
not exist in your area.

ISBN-13: 978-0-373-27646-2

5 MINUTES TO MARRIAGE

Copyright © 2009 by Harlequin Books S.A.

Visit Silhouette Books at www.eHarlequin.com

Printed in U.S.A.

Books by Carla Cassidy

Silhouette Romantic Suspense

One of the Good Guys #531
Try to Remember #560
Fugitive Father #604
Behind Closed Doors #778
**Reluctant Wife* #850
**Reluctant Dad* #856
**Her Counterfeit Husband* #885
**Code Name: Cowboy* #902
**Rodeo Dad* #934
In a Heartbeat #1005
**Imminent Danger* #1018
*Strangers When
    We Married* #1046
†*Man on a Mission* #1077
Born of Passion #1094
†*Once Forbidden...* #1115
†*To Wed and Protect* #1126
†*Out of Exile* #1149
*Secrets of a
    Pregnant Princess* #1166
††*Last Seen...* #1233
††*Dead Certain* #1250
††*Trace Evidence* #1261
††*Manhunt* #1294

‡*Protecting the Princess* #1345
‡*Defending the
    Rancher's Daughter* #1376
‡*The Bodyguard's Promise* #1419
‡*The Bodyguard's Return* #1447
‡*Safety in Numbers* #1463
‡*Snowbound with
    the Bodyguard* #1521
‡*Natural-Born Protector* #1527
A Hero of Her Own #1548
‡*The Rancher Bodyguard* #1551
5 Minutes to Marriage #1576

*Mustang, Montana
**Sisters
†The Delaney Heirs
††Cherokee Corners
‡Wild West Bodyguards

CARLA CASSIDY

is an award-winning author who has written more than fifty books for Silhouette Books. In 1995, she won Best Silhouette Romance from *Romantic Times BOOKreviews* for *Anything for Danny*. In 1998, she also won a Career Achievement Award for Best Innovative Series.

Carla believes the only thing better than curling up with a good book to read is sitting down at the computer with a good story to write. She's looking forward to writing many more books and bringing hours of pleasure to readers.

Prologue

He stood on the curb across the street from the casino with its glittering lights and flashy marquee, and the ball of hatred inside him expanded to make him half-breathless.

Harold Rothchild owned this casino, the same Harold Rothchild who had built his fortune on the destruction and blood of others, the same Harold who had destroyed his life.

A small smile curved his lips. Poor Harold's life had taken a turn for the worse. "And it's all because of me," he whispered to himself.

He'd killed Harold's daughter and he now had in his possession the invaluable Tears of the Quetzal diamond ring. He'd done everything he'd set out to do, but as he started at the grand entrance of the casino, he realized it wasn't enough.

That was the funny thing about revenge—just when you thought you'd achieved it, that gnawing hunger for more rose inside you.

He felt it now, burgeoning in his chest, and he clenched his hands into fists at his sides. Rage. It roared through him like a hot wind, stirring his need to inflict more pain, more heartache.

He wasn't through with the Rothchilds, not yet, not by a long shot. He wouldn't be through until Harold Rothchild and his family fell to their knees and wept for all they had lost.

Chapter 1

The evening began with such promise. The house was in order, the kids had been bathed and dressed in matching outfits and Jack Cortland was looking forward to his date.

He'd met Heidi Gray in the grocery store on one of his rare trips into town. The sophisticated, attractive blonde had smiled at him, and before they'd left the produce section, they'd made a date. Since that time they'd been out three times, and tonight was the first time she would meet his children.

Ten minutes before she was set to arrive, he sat down with his two sons on the sofa. Four-year-old

Mick sat on one side of him and three-year-old David was on the other.

"Now, boys, this is a really important night. I want you both to be on your best behavior and be nice to Miss Heidi when she gets here," he said.

"Heidi tighty whitey," Mick exclaimed.

"Heidi tighty whitey," David echoed, and the two broke into gales of laughter.

"Now, now, boys," Jack said in an effort to gain control, but it was too late. Their giggles increased in volume, and Jack sat and waited until finally they'd worn their giggles out.

"I do not want to hear you say that again," Jack said as firmly as possible.

David frowned at him. "Bad Jack," he said. "No yelling."

"I wasn't yelling," Jack protested, and then sighed. "Why don't the two of you go play in your room until our guest arrives."

He watched as they raced out of the living room and down the hallway toward the bedroom. When they disappeared out of sight, he released a sigh of exhaustion.

The boys had been in his custody for a little over four months, ever since their mother, his ex-wife, Candace, had been murdered. And in those months he'd realized they were undisciplined, wild and had absolutely zero respect for him.

Jack knew how to beat a rhythm on the drums to

stir the blood. He could sing the rock and roll that was in his soul. He knew how to entertain a stadium of fans with his music. There had been a time not so long ago when he'd also known how to drink and drug himself into oblivion, but he didn't know anything about parenting.

He pulled himself up from the sofa and went into the kitchen, where the delicious scents of pot roast wafted in the air. Betty, his cook, stood before the sink, washing the last of the dishes before she left for the day.

"Everything is done and in the oven waiting to go on the table," she said as she turned away from the sink and dried her hands on a towel.

"Sure you don't want to stick around?" Jack asked hopefully.

She gave him one of her dour gazes. "I told you when you hired me that I cook and that's it. I don't serve, I don't clean house and I definitely don't babysit." She grabbed her purse from the top of the counter. "I'll see you tomorrow morning, Mr. Cortland."

As she headed for the back door, Jack squashed the panic that threatened to rise in his chest. He told himself that the night was going to be a rousing success.

He wandered into the dining room, where Betty had set the table with the good dishes and linen napkins. It was probably a mistake to share the meal with both his date and his sons, but it was important to him that whatever woman he invited into his life knew that his sons were part of the package deal.

For a year following his divorce from Candace, Jack had rarely seen his sons. Candace has spent much of that year globe-trotting, and Jack had been in no condition, either financially or emotionally, to chase after her.

When Candace had been murdered the boys had come to live with him, but Jack knew Harold Rothchild, Candace's father, was just waiting for him to make a mistake so he could swoop in and take the boys away.

Jack's stomach tightened at the thought of Harold. There was no question the wealthy, powerful Las Vegas mogul wanted his grandsons, but the only way he could take custody away from Jack was to prove that he was an unfit father. Jack was doing everything in his power to make sure that didn't happen. He was determined to be the best father he could be.

The doorbell rang, signaling the arrival of Heidi, and Jack hurried to the door to welcome her. From the direction of the bedroom came the sounds of the boys laughing, and once again he mentally muttered a prayer that the evening went well.

The first thirty minutes were relatively successful. On their previous dates Jack had found Heidi to be a good conversationalist, and it didn't hurt that she was jaw-droppingly gorgeous. He was male enough to enjoy the scent of her perfume in the air and the hint of cleavage that her V-neck blouse offered him.

After a brief introduction to the boys, they returned to playing in their room, giving Jack and Heidi time alone.

When it was time to move into the dining room for the meal, there were several minutes of chaos as Jack got the boys settled in their booster seats at the table, then hurried into the kitchen to bring out the meal that Betty had prepared.

Pot roast and potatoes, broccoli florets with cheese, homemade dinner rolls and a Jell-O salad all went to the table, and after filling the boys' plates, Jack returned to his seat.

"This looks yummy," Heidi said. "Did you do all this?"

"I wish I could take credit for it, but no. I have a local woman who comes in to cook for us." He smiled at her, then blinked as a piece of cheesy broccoli smacked her chest and slowly slid downward before falling into the vee of her blouse.

Mick giggled.

Jack stared at his son in horror. "Mick!" He turned back to Heidi. "I'm so sorry."

Another cheese-covered floret struck her in the head, and this time it was David who laughed uproariously. Suddenly the broccoli was flying and

Jack was yelling. Heidi jumped up from the table in an effort to escape the onslaught of food, her features tight with aggravation.

"Mick, David! Stop it right now," Jack exclaimed.

"Bad Jack," Mick yelled.

"I'm out of here," Heidi exclaimed. "I wasn't sure that I was at a place in my life to be an instant mother, and now I know the answer. I'm definitely not ready for this. Your children are undisciplined little boys, and you all need more than I can offer." She grabbed her purse and marched out of the dining room. Jack ran after her, muttering apologies that she obviously didn't want to hear.

As she slammed out of the front door, Jack leaned against the wall and closed his eyes. She was right. His boys were unruly animals, and he didn't know what to do about it, but something had to be done.

He could just see the tabloid headlines now: "Rock Star Children Belong in a Zoo." He hoped Heidi wasn't the type to cash in by selling the tale of the evening to the tabloids.

By ten that evening the boys had finally fallen asleep, David on the living-room floor and Mick on the sofa. Jack carried them into their room and put them into their beds, then returned to the living room and called his lifelong buddy, Kent Goodall.

Within fifteen minutes Kent was at the house and the two men were seated at the kitchen table sipping coffee as Jack told Kent about the disastrous date.

"I need help," Jack said. "Heidi was right. The boys are out of control, and I don't know how to fix things."

Kent swept a strand of his long blond hair behind one pierced ear. "I know a woman, a professional nanny. Her name is Marisa Perez, and she lives right here in Las Vegas."

"How do you know her?" Jack asked. Kent had no children. He wasn't even married.

"Remember the woman I dated? Ramona with the big hair and bigger chest? She's a friend of Marisa's. Last I heard Marisa was saving money to open up her own nanny agency."

Jack frowned. He didn't want to just invite anyone into his home and into the lives of his sons. As he recalled, Ramona with the big hair also had a pea brain. She'd been working as a showgirl in one of the casinos. He wasn't sure being a friend to Ramona was necessarily a good qualification for interacting with his children.

"I'm not sure Ramona vouching for somebody makes me comfortable," he finally said.

Kent grinned. "Trust me, I hear you, but it wouldn't hurt for you to interview Marisa and see if she's everything Ramona said she was. I'll call Ramona and get her number for you."

Jack wrapped his hands around his coffee mug and nodded. "I have to do something. If Harold gets wind of how badly I'm mangling the parenting stuff, he'll have me back in court fighting for custody." A painful knot formed in Jack's chest as he thought of the possibility of losing his boys.

For the next few minutes the men talked music and bands. When Kent and Jack had been teenagers, they'd formed a band that had played local clubs and at weddings. The band had been successful on a regional level, but Jack had hungered for more.

At the age of twenty-two he'd left Las Vegas for Los Angeles and eventually had hooked up with a group of musicians who had become the rock band Creation.

While Jack had ridden the rise of fame and fortune, then eventually crashed and burned, Kent had remained in Las Vegas with his band members, playing local gigs whenever they could get them.

It was after midnight when Kent finally left, and Jack had finished clearing the dishes from the dining-room table.

When he was finished he went down the hallway toward the bedrooms. The first one he stopped in was the boys' bedroom, and he stood in the doorway and stared at his sons.

Mick slept on his side, his legs and arms curled into a fetal position. David lay sprawled on his back, arms and legs thrown to his sides as if he'd fallen asleep in the middle of a leap off a building.

A surge of tenderness flowed through him as he watched them sleep. The love he felt for his sons was like nothing he'd ever experienced before.

Although he didn't want to think ill of the dead, Candace had possessed the maternal instincts of a rock. Jack had hoped that the birth of the boys would somehow domesticate the wild, beautiful woman he'd married—and for a while it had worked. But it didn't take long for the novelty of motherhood to wear off and for their marriage to self-destruct.

The boys had so many strikes against them. A mother who had been murdered and a father who was a recovering addict and knew nothing about being a dad.

They needed somebody else in their life, a nanny who could teach them how to be good boys—and the sooner the better.

"You are stupid to even consider this," Marisa Perez said aloud to herself as she drove down the dusty Nevada road in the direction of Jack Cortland's ranch.

He'd called her earlier that morning and asked her about her services as a nanny. Against her better judgment she'd agreed to meet with him at his house.

It had been big news when Jack had moved back to his family home two years ago following a very public divorce from Candace Rothchild.

For years Jack and Candace had been a favorite topic of gossip in the tabloids. Their lifestyle of excess and drugs and alcohol had been legendary.

The public had loved stories of the hard-rock star and his beautiful heiress wife.

From everything Marisa knew about Jack Cortland, she was not impressed. She glanced out her side window, passing land that her parents probably owned.

Like Candace, Marisa had come from wealth, but unlike Candace, Marisa had decided early on that she wanted to make her own way. She didn't want to work for the family in their real estate ventures. What she loved was working with children.

She tightened her grip on the steering wheel as she turned into the long, dusty driveway that led to the Cortland ranch.

This visit was more to satisfy her curiosity than for any other reason. Since moving back here Jack had kept a low profile, rarely being seen out of his home.

She'd read the stories about Candace's tragic murder and knew there were two little boys in Jack's custody. More than anything she'd been driven to come out here to check on those boys.

She might not think much of Jack Cortland as a person, but he had a low, deep voice that could weaken the knees of a soldier. After talking to him on the phone that morning, it had taken her several minutes to get that sexy voice out of her head.

The farmhouse came into view, and as she pulled up front and parked, she saw a towheaded tot wearing only a diaper racing across the grass and heading toward a large barn in the distance.

Marisa turned off her engine and expected at any moment some adult to come running out of the house to collect the child. When that didn't immediately happen, she jumped out of her car and hurried toward the little tot.

"Hi," she said when she caught up with him.

He stopped and smiled at her, and her heart crunched in her chest. He looked like a little angel with his pale hair and bright blue eyes. "Hi," he replied.

"What's your name?" she asked.

"David." He glanced toward the barn, as if eager to be on his way.

"I'm Marisa. You want to play a game?" His eyes lit up and he nodded. "Do you know how to jump on one foot?" He nodded again and began to jump up and down. "Let's see who can jump on one foot all the way to the house."

He took off, alternately hopping and running. Marisa followed after him, silently seething over the fact that a baby was outside alone with no adult supervision in sight.

David's laughter rang in the air as he hurried toward the house with Marisa at his heels. They had just reached the porch when the front door exploded open and Jack Cortland flew outside.

His gray eyes were wide with alarm as he took

the stairs of the porch two at a time. "David! Thank God." He grabbed the boy up in his arms, then stared at Marisa, panic still gleaming in his eyes.

She said nothing, merely stood drinking in the sight of the infamous Jack. She'd expected a man who looked dissipated, a man with sallow skin and the lines of debauchery slashed deep in his face. Instead his dark hair gleamed richly in the overhead sunshine. He sported a healthy tan and arm muscles that looked as if he wasn't a stranger to hard work.

He was hot…and for just a few seconds, Marisa forgot what she was doing here. It was only when David squealed in protest and struggled to get out of his father's arms that her brain reengaged.

"I'd say you have a problem with basic safety issues," she said.

"He's Houdini reincarnated," Jack said with obvious frustration. "I assume you're Marisa?" She gave him a brief nod, and he gestured her toward the front door. "Welcome to the zoo."

"I need to get some things from my car," she said. "I jumped out when I saw David racing across the grass and no adult in sight." She couldn't keep the thick disapproval from her voice.

"I didn't know he'd escaped," he replied with a grimace. "Get whatever you need and come on in." He didn't wait for her reply, but instead disappeared into the house.

Marisa headed back to her car and tried to still the

crazy butterflies that had gone dancing in her stomach at the sight of him. She couldn't remember when just looking at a man had caused such a visceral reaction. Certainly when she'd first met Patrick she hadn't felt the burst of heat that the sight of Jack had evoked.

The man was a mess, she reminded herself as she grabbed her purse and briefcase from the passenger seat.

Still, as she headed toward the front door she steeled herself against his obvious attractiveness. She was here to contemplate a job and nothing more. She had a boyfriend, her life was on track and the last thing she needed was for some thirty-year-old drummer with a disastrous history rocking her world.

She swept through the front door and into a small entry and then into a large living room that was obviously the heart of the house.

Jack stood in the center of the room, which was littered with toys and kids' clothes and had the faint scent of a dirty diaper. The boys were wrestling on the floor, and as Jack looked at her, once again his soft gray eyes held an appeal. "I need help."

She felt her resolve not to get involved fading away. He looked so utterly helpless in the midst of the chaos. "Is there someplace we can sit and chat?" she asked.

"Boys, why don't you go to your room and play," Jack said.

David jumped up and smiled at Marisa. "Watch," he said, then hopped on one foot down the hallway. The other boy followed his brother, and the two of them disappeared from view.

Jack swept a handful of blocks and toy trucks off the sofa and gestured her to have a seat. Then he sat in the chair opposite the sofa.

"I've had the boys in my custody for almost four months," he said. "They came to me undisciplined and wild, and as you can see, I haven't managed to change things much in the time that I've had them."

"Exactly what are you looking for from me, Mr. Cortland?" she asked.

"Jack, please make it Jack." He smiled, but the gesture didn't quite erase the worry from his eyes. "Isn't it obvious that I need somebody to train the boys and to teach them how to behave?"

Marisa didn't think Jack was ready to hear that. In her experience it was usually the parents who needed training, not the children.

At the moment she saw nothing of the hard-rock star. What she saw was a concerned father worried about his sons. She held on to her heart. There was something about Jack Cortland that made her think that if she allowed it, it would take about five minutes for her to fall crazy in love with him.

But of course she wouldn't allow it. She wasn't even sure she was going to take this job. Just because Jack had beautiful gray eyes fringed with sinfully long lashes, just because he had lips that looked as if they could drive a woman wild didn't mean she was eager to work as a nanny for him.

She opened her briefcase and pulled out a sheath of papers. "Here are my credentials and references," she said as she held them out toward him.

He waved his hand in the air. "Trust me, I've already checked you out, Ms. Perez. I wasn't about to allow just anyone into my home with my boys." He shot her a level gaze. "You graduated from college with a degree in early childhood education. You're twenty-seven years old, live alone and you're particularly close to your aunt Rita, who has worked as an FBI agent for the last twenty years."

Marisa raised an eyebrow. "Please, call me Marisa," she said, impressed by the fact that he'd done his homework where she was concerned. "How many other people do you have working for you here in the home?" she asked. "I need to know who the children interact with on a daily basis."

"I have a cook who comes in the morning and leaves right after she fixes the evening meal. Other than that, it's pretty much just me. The nanny Candace had used for the boys got another job."

"No housekeeper?" she asked.

One corner of his mouth turned up in a rueful grin as he looked pointedly around the room. "If I had a housekeeper, I would have definitely fired her by now."

"You understand this would be a live-in position," she said.

"There's a spare bedroom across from the boys' room. You'd have your own private bath and of course free access to the rest of the house." He leaned forward in his chair. "Tell me you'll take the job, Marisa. You have no idea how important this is to me."

But she did see how important it was to him. A frantic desperation shone from his eyes, something that looked remarkably like fear.

There was more going on here than just his need for her to teach the boys to be well-behaved. She was definitely intrigued.

The fee she collected from this job would put the final dollars in her bank account that she needed to start her business, but she had no idea how far Jack had come from the bad-boy rocker he had once been. Was this really a man she wanted to work for?

"Okay," she heard herself saying before she even knew she'd made a conscious decision. "But I have a condition."

"Just name it," he exclaimed.

"We agree to a weeklong probationary period. If at the end of that week you wish to terminate me, or I decide to leave, then you pay me for the week and I'm on my way. At the end of that week if we're both agreeable, then I have a contract to sign that will assure me two months here."

"Just two months?" he asked.

"I'm a troubleshooter. I only work temporary positions. If you're looking for somebody for long-term, then when I finish my two months I'll help you hire somebody for a permanent position."

"Sounds reasonable to me. When can you start?"

"Tomorrow morning around nine?"

"Perfect," he said with a sigh of relief. She stood and so did he.

She was far too aware of him just behind her as she walked back to the front door. She turned back to him, finding him standing ridiculously close to her. The scent of him washed over her, a clean scent coupled with the faint remnants of a spicy cologne.

She stepped back, her breath catching in her chest as that crazy surge of heat swept through her. He held out his hand, and she stared at it for a long moment, almost afraid to touch him, afraid of how that touch might make her feel.

"I'll see you in the morning," she said as he awkwardly dropped his hand to his side. She flew out the door and hurried toward her car.

Dear God, what was wrong with her? She was acting like some silly, empty-headed fan—and she hadn't even liked his music or his band.

She was doing this strictly for the kids. It was obvious they needed some loving attention and a firm hand. Still, as she thought about moving into

Jack Cortland's home the next morning, she couldn't help feeling that it might just be the biggest mistake she'd ever made in her life.

Chapter 2

"What's he like?" Marisa's aunt Rita asked. Rita had invited Marisa and Marisa's current boyfriend, Patrick Moore, for dinner that evening. They were all seated around the dining table in Rita's apartment.

Marisa picked up her glass of ice water, as if needing the cold against her skin as she talked about Jack Cortland. "Desperate," she replied. "The little boys are a mess and from all appearances are the ones running things."

"I still don't like it," Patrick exclaimed. "That man has a terrible reputation. I don't like the idea of you living in that house with him."

Marisa smiled at the handsome man across from her at the table. "Initially it's just for a week. If I see behavior that makes me uncomfortable, then after that week I'll be done."

There were times she thought Patrick was too good to be true. Not only was he incredibly handsome and charming but he also had a good job as an accountant and seemed to have fallen head over heels in love with her.

They'd been dating only a couple of weeks, but Patrick had already made it clear that he believed she was the woman he wanted to spend the rest of his life with.

Although Marisa liked him a great deal, she wasn't about to fall into a hot, passionate affair with a man she'd been dating only a brief time. She'd done that once before in her life, and the results had been devastating.

She took a sip of her water and wondered why thoughts of a hot affair automatically brought a vision of Jack to her mind.

"I was a fan of Jack's band for a while," Patrick said. "Creation did some awesome songs, but once he married Candace Rothchild the band seemed to go straight downhill."

"Such a shame about her," Marisa said. She looked at her aunt. "You were working that murder case for a while, weren't you?"

"Still am," Rita replied. "Unfortunately, there

aren't many leads to follow." Rita shook her head. "I can't imagine having to bury a child, even a child who was thirty years old at the time of her murder."

"It doesn't seem to have slowed down her father. What's he on now—his third or fourth wife?" Patrick asked.

"Third wife," Rita replied. "This current one is a former showgirl considerably younger than him. Rumor has it that the thrill is gone and the marriage is in trouble."

"I'm sorry that Harold lost a daughter, but I'm even sorrier that David and Mick lost their mother," Marisa said.

Patrick smiled ruefully. "From all accounts, she wasn't much of a mother."

"I know, but I still feel bad for those little boys," Marisa replied.

"Just don't get too emotionally involved," Rita said with a gentle smile.

Marisa laughed. "Aunt Rita, I've been a nanny for quite some time now. I know how to separate myself from my little charges. I never lose track of the fact that I'm only in their lives temporarily."

Rita was the only person on the face of the earth who knew what had happened to Marisa in college. Eventually if she and Patrick decided to marry, she'd have to tell him before any vows were exchanged. But it was far too early in their relationship for deep, dark secrets to be exposed.

The rest of the dinner was pleasant, and when they were finished Patrick excused himself from the table and disappeared down the hallway toward the bathroom while Marisa and Rita began to clear the table.

"I like him," Rita said as she rinsed off one of the dinner plates. This was only the second time Patrick and Rita had shared any real quality time together. Rita had entertained them over dinner a week earlier.

"He is great, isn't he?" Marisa handed her another plate. "He couldn't wait to get to know you better. He knows how important you are to me."

Although Marisa's parents were lovely people, they'd never really understood their daughter's desire to make her own way in the world rather than follow them into the very lucrative family real estate business.

Marisa had always been particularly close to her father's sister, Rita. It had been Rita who Marisa had confided in when her world had fallen apart in college.

"How are you doing?" Marisa asked and gestured to the bandage on the side of Rita's head. She and Jenna Rothchild had been kidnapped, and Rita had suffered a gunshot wound to the head. It had rendered her unconscious, and although she and Jenna had managed to get away neither of them had been able to identify the man responsible or why they had been kidnapped in the first place.

"I'm okay—a little headache now and then, but that's all," Rita replied. "You're taking things slow with Patrick?"

"Absolutely. I want to marry once in my life. I'm not about to jump into anything too intense too fast."

Rita smiled. "I think Patrick has other ideas. He seems quite smitten with you."

At that moment he walked back into the kitchen and any further conversation with him as the topic halted.

After cleaning up the kitchen, the three of them moved into the living room where the conversation revolved around Las Vegas life, Patrick's work and a new casino that had opened in town. Rita never discussed her work, but she was a charming hostess who kept the conversation flowing until Patrick and Marisa decided to call it a night.

It was just after nine when Patrick pulled up in front of the small house Marisa rented. "I like your aunt," he said.

"She liked you, too," Marisa replied.

"What's not to like?" He flashed her a bright smile.

"I'd invite you in, but I really want to get a good night's sleep before the morning," she said as he parked the car.

"Am I going to see you at all over the next week?" he asked.

"Probably not," Marisa admitted. "The first week

in a new position is always pretty intense. But it's just for a week, Patrick." She opened the passenger door and got out.

Patrick got out of the car as well and fell into step next to her. He grabbed her hand in his as they walked to her front porch. "And what happens after the first week? What if you take the position for the next couple months? Does that mean I won't be able to see you the whole time?"

She disentangled her hand from his to reach into her purse for her keys. "Not at all. If Jack Cortland and I agree that he needs my services for that long, then I always make sure I have most weekends off."

She unlocked her door then turned back to face him. "Good night, Patrick." She reached up and kissed him on his smooth cheek, but he quickly pulled her into his arms for a real kiss.

It was pleasant, but it didn't curl her toes or weaken her knees. When the kiss ended he reluctantly released her. "Then I guess I'll see you in a week or so?"

"I'll call you and let you know how things are going," she replied.

"You know I'll be waiting for your calls," he replied.

She watched as he walked back to his car. He was a man who could easily turn female heads. Tall and slim, with the dark features of his Hispanic heritage, he always dressed with an understated elegance and looked both handsome and successful.

Minutes later as she undressed in her bedroom she thought of that kiss and Patrick. Maybe one of the reasons she was attracted to Patrick was because there weren't wild fireworks when they kissed, there wasn't that sizzle that came from a simple touch and the breathlessness of a mere glance.

She'd experienced that crazy hot passion once in her life and never wanted it again. It had destroyed her life, and the thought of feeling that way again frightened her.

She pulled her red silk nightgown over her head, turned out the light and crawled into bed. Maybe real love was just that faint warmth that filled her when Patrick smiled at her or the quiet friendship they were building together.

She frowned as she thought of Jack Cortland. So what was it about him that had caused that sizzle inside her? Why did a man she had little respect for, given his past, fill her with a wild sense of anticipation at the very thought of seeing him again?

Jack worked until almost three in the morning cleaning the house. The boys had finally fallen asleep around eleven. He'd moved them into their bedroom, then had tackled the living room with a vengeance.

Toys went back into the boys' room, dirty plates and cups carried back to the kitchen. He polished and washed and vacuumed until the room looked presentable. Then he went into the guest room that Marisa would call home and cleaned it as well.

It had needed to be done for the past couple months, but the days were so full with keeping the boys occupied and trying to oversee the work being done on the ranch. By the time the boys fell asleep at night Jack was comatose, and cleaning was the last thing on his mind.

He'd considered hiring more help but had put it off, hoping to get the boys better acclimated to him before bringing other people into their lives.

When he finally fell into bed he thought sleep would come quickly, but instead he found himself thinking of Marisa Perez.

He hadn't expected her to be so sexy. Even though he'd known before he'd met her that she was twenty-seven years old, he'd expected a maternal type, someone who was overweight and not particularly attractive.

Marisa had been more than attractive. Her long, dark brown hair had sparkled with honey highlights and dark, sexy lashes fringed her large chocolate brown eyes. She had the bone structure of a model, but her body wasn't model thin; rather, it was lush with curves in all the right places.

He'd eventually fallen asleep and dreamed of her…and in those dreams she'd been soft and yielding in his arms. Her kisses had stirred him like none had ever done.

He awoke at dawn and hurried into the shower, eager to get dressed and maybe choke down a cup of coffee before the boys awoke.

Betty wouldn't arrive for another hour so he made the coffee, poured himself a cup and sat at the table, trying not to remember the dreams that had bordered on downright erotic.

He breathed in the peace and quiet of the morning and stared out the window where his herd of cattle grazed on whatever vegetation they could find in the hard, dry earth.

His father had raised cattle here, as had his father before him. Jack's dad had wanted Jack to follow in his footsteps, to take over the ranch and continue producing quality cattle. He'd wanted Jack to live by the values they'd tried to teach him instead of the ones Jack had learned on his way to fame and fortune.

It would always grieve Jack that both his parents had died before he had returned here. Worse than that, he suspected that they had died brokenhearted by the bad choices their son had made in his life as a rock star.

He wouldn't make the same mistakes now. He wanted his boys to grow up and be proud of him. He wanted to give them a solid foundation of love and good values. More than anything he wanted to be the man his parents had known that he could be.

By eight-thirty Jack looked forward to the arrival

of Marisa. The boys had been fed their breakfast and were dressed in clean clothes.

The living room was still relatively clean, and the boys were playing quietly with their trucks in the middle of the floor.

Jack was grateful that he was going to get some parenting tips from Marisa, but he also recognized that his interest in her wasn't solely that of a father needing help with his kids.

It had been a man's interest that had kept him awake the night before, and it had been a shocking desire for her that had filled his dreams, reminding him that he'd been alone for a very long time.

At exactly nine o'clock his doorbell rang and he hurried to greet her, surprised that his heart was pumping harder than it had in months.

He opened the door, and she offered him a bright smile that made him believe that this was going to be a very fine day. "Good morning, come on in."

As she walked past him into the living room he caught her scent, a floral spice that seemed to shoot right to his brain. "What a pleasant surprise," she said. "You've cleaned."

He gave her a sheepish grin. "I didn't realize how bad things had gotten until I saw them through your eyes. Here, let me take that." He gestured to the suitcase she held in her hand. "I'll just take it to your room."

"Thanks," she replied.

He took the case and hurried down the hall. When he returned she was in the middle of the floor with David and Mick. The boys were showing her the trucks that were their favorite toys.

"So how does this work?" he asked. "You just teach them what they need to do?"

She smiled and rose from the floor with a sinuous grace. "It's not quite that easy, Jack. What I'd like to do this morning is just kind of sit back and observe what would be a normal morning for you and the boys. Then at lunch we'll sit down with a game plan."

"Oh, okay." He shoved his hands in his jeans pockets and stared down at his sons, then back at her. "All of a sudden I'm feeling very self-conscious," he admitted.

At that moment Mick hit David with one of the trucks, and within seconds both boys were crying and Jack was yelling. He grabbed Mick up into his arms. "You don't hit, Mick. That's not nice."

"Bad Jack," Mick cried and wiggled to get out of his arms.

"Bad Jack," David yelled, obviously forgetting that it was his brother, not his father, who had hit him in the head.

"Both of you go to your room," Jack exclaimed as he set Mick back on his feet. "Go on. You're both in trouble."

As the boys went running down the hallway, Jack

slicked a hand through his hair in frustration then looked at Marisa. "I handled that badly, right?"

"We'll talk at lunch," she said, her beautiful features giving nothing away of her emotions.

The morning passed excruciatingly slow for Jack. The boys seemed to be on their worst behavior, and he was overly conscious of Marisa watching his every move.

Then, right before lunchtime, while he was in the bathroom with Mick, David climbed through the window in his bedroom and snuck out of the house. As soon as he realized what had happened, Jack raced down the front porch to grab David. Marisa and Mick stood in the doorway and watched him.

Jack was exhausted and his patience was wearing thin. He hadn't hired the lovely nanny to stand around and observe. She was supposed to be fixing things, not watching from the sidelines.

When Betty announced that lunch was ready, Jack had never been so happy for a meal. He set the boys in their booster seats at the dining-room table then gestured Marisa into the chair opposite his as he introduced her to the cook.

"About time you did something," she said to Jack, then glared at Marisa. "I don't babysit, and I don't clean. I don't leave this kitchen except to serve the breakfast and lunch meals. I don't serve dinner. I just cook. That's all I do."

"That's good to know," Marisa replied with a friendly smile. Betty harrumphed and disappeared back into the kitchen.

"I pay her for her cooking skills, not her sparkling personality," Jack said with a dry chuckle.

Marisa laughed, and the sound of her laughter filled a space in him that had been silent for a very long time.

He couldn't remember the last time he'd shared any laughter with anyone. For the past couple months everything had been so tense; the stakes had been so incredibly high.

"One of the first things we need to address is David's ability to escape out any door and window," she said. David smiled at her, his mouth smeared with mustard from his ham sandwich. "You need to purchase childproof locks for every door," she continued.

"I agree. It's only been in the past week or so that he's developed this new skill," Jack replied.

The afternoon sun drifting through the window played on those golden highlights in her hair, making it look incredibly soft and touchable. Her lipstick had worn off by midmorning, but she had naturally plump, rosy lips that he found incredibly sexy.

"What's bedtime like?" she asked.

"Bedtime?" Memories of the visions he'd had of her the night before in his sleep exploded in his head, and he felt a warm wave seep through his veins.

"Do the boys have a regular bedtime?"

He shoved the visions away. "It's regular in that their bedtime is whenever they fall asleep."

"And they fall asleep in their beds?"

"They sleep wherever they happen to fall," he replied.

"They're bright, beautiful boys," she said.

Her words swelled a ball of pride in his chest. "Thanks. I just want them to be good boys as well."

"Good boys," David quipped and nodded his head with an angelic smile, then threw a potato chip in Jack's direction.

After lunch the boys played for a little while, then both of them fell asleep on the floor. Jack carried each of them into their room, put them in bed for their afternoon nap and then returned to where Marisa sat on the sofa.

He sat on the opposite end from her, close enough that he could smell the enticing scent of her perfume. "They should sleep for about an hour," he said.

"What's in the barn?"

He blinked at the question that seemed to come out of nowhere. "What?"

"Both times David got out of the house he was heading for the barn. What's inside?"

"A small recording studio, memorabilia from my old band, my drum set." He shrugged. "My past."

"You miss it?" she asked.

He considered the question before immediately replying. "Some of it," he admitted. "I miss making music, but I don't miss everything that came with it. Why do you ask?"

Her dark eyes considered him thoughtfully. "I need to know that you're in this for the long haul, that the number one priority in your life is your boys. I don't want to spend a month or two of my time helping you here only to have you decide fatherhood is too boring and you'd rather be out on the road making music."

There was a touch of censure in her voice that stirred a hint of irritation inside him. "Nothing in my life means more to me than David and Mick. When Candace and I divorced I rarely got to see the boys. Usually the only time I saw them or heard about them was if they were mentioned in an article in a tabloid." He exhaled sharply. "I'm sorry Candace is dead, but I'm glad the boys are with me now—and I intend to do right by them not just for a month or two but for the rest of their lives."

Warmth leaped into her eyes, and that warmth shot straight into the pit of his stomach. He couldn't remember the last time a woman had affected him so intensely. He wanted to reach out and tangle his hands in her long hair. He wanted to press his lips against hers and taste her.

"It's not going to be easy to turn things around here," she warned.

He smiled. "Over the past couple of years I've fought some pretty strong personal demons. Two little boys aren't going to get the best of me."

"'Bad Jack.' Where did they learn that?"

Jack's smile fell and he frowned instead. "I suppose from Candace. They refuse to call me anything but that."

She leaned back against the cushion. "I hate to tell you this, Jack, but what we need to work on most is your behavior. Those boys are crying out for positive attention and boundaries."

"I'm game," he replied.

"Good." She stood. "I'm going to go unload some things from my car."

He jumped up. "Need help?"

"No, I can handle it." Her eyes twinkled with humor. "Besides, you'd better save your strength. You're going to need it."

He followed her to the front door and watched as she went down the stairs, her hips swaying invitingly beneath the navy slacks she wore.

The background check he'd done on her had told him a lot of things about her, but it hadn't told him what he wanted to know at this moment.

Did she have a boyfriend? Was she in some kind of a committed relationship? Would he be a total fool to get involved with the woman he'd hired as a nanny?

He scoffed at his own thoughts. He'd be a real fool to think that a woman like Marisa would have any interest in a man like him. He was nothing but a washed-up rocker who she'd already seen as useless and ineffectual.

She was bright and beautiful and he could want her, but it was a desire he didn't intend to follow through on. She was here for his boys and that was enough for him…it had to be enough.

Chapter 3

As the day wore on Marisa told herself again and again that she was here for David and Mick and nothing more.

She could not allow herself to get caught up in her overwhelming attraction to Jack. She refused to allow herself to admit that she liked him. Still, she could admire the man he was now despite the fact that she had a feeling she would have disrespected the man he had once been.

During the afternoon she met Kent Goodall, who was one of Jack's closest friends. He was a tall, blond man who told her he used to play bass in a band with Jack when they'd been teenagers. He was affable but didn't stay long.

She also met the two ranch hands who worked for Jack. Sam and Max Burrow were brothers who had the dark leathery skin of men who had spent their entire lives out in the elements. They appeared quiet and uncomfortable as they stepped into the kitchen through the back door.

Sam had been sent to town to pick up childproof locks for the windows and doors in the house. Once he gave them to Jack the two disappeared back outside.

As Jack put them on, Marisa sat with the boys on the sofa and read them a story. David snuggled next to her on one side and Mick on the other. She had already lost her heart to the boys, who were definitely rambunctious but also responding to her gentle guidance.

It was at bedtime that things got wild as Marisa instructed Jack to put the boys to bed in their room. Every few minutes the boys came out of the bedroom and Jack carried them back in and tucked them in once again.

The boys screamed and cried, and Jack shot Marisa frustrated looks as he carried them back to their beds. It was after one in the morning when he returned from their bedroom and flopped on the sofa. Silence reigned.

"It will be easier tomorrow night," she said.

He scowled at her. "I hope that's a promise."

She smiled. "I forgot to mention that there are

going to be moments in this process when you'll probably hate me."

His scowl lifted, and he offered her a sexy half grin that ripped at her heart. "I'm not mad at you. I'm mad at myself for not doing this when I first got them here." His smile fell, and he gazed at her curiously. "Why aren't you married with a dozen kids of your own? It's obvious you love children."

The question pierced through her, bringing forth a longing that she knew would never really be satisfied. "I'm young. I have plenty of time for all that in the future," she replied airily.

"Are you seeing somebody?"

She nodded. "Yes, I have somebody I'm seeing." She needed to let him know that, but she also needed to remind herself. Patrick. Patrick was the man in her life at the moment and she definitely needed to remember that.

She stood, suddenly needing to escape from Jack. "Time to call it a night," she said. "Tomorrow is a brand-new day."

He got up as well, and together they walked down the hallway toward the bedrooms. "You'll let me know if you need anything?" he asked as they stopped in front of the room where she'd be staying.

"I'm sure I'll be fine," she replied. She released a soft gasp as he reached out and grabbed one of her hands.

"I just want to tell you how glad I am that you're

here," he murmured huskily. "You have no idea how grateful I am."

Those crazy butterflies winged through her stomach, and she pulled her hand from his, uncomfortable by the way his touch made her feel.

"Good night, Jack." She escaped into the bedroom and closed the door behind her.

What on earth was wrong with her? She had to get hold of herself and stop thinking about Jack as a man rather than a client.

She moved into the bathroom to get ready for bed. Her attraction to him wasn't just a physical one. There had been moments in the day when she'd sensed a deep loneliness inside him—one that had called to something deep inside her.

She was intrigued as well. There was a desperation about him that went far beyond a father concerned with his sons' behavior.

The light of dawn awoke her the next morning, but she remained in bed for several long minutes, going over the things she intended to accomplish that day.

She wondered why Jack hadn't already hired a nanny or a babysitter for the kids. Surely he needed to be outside doing things to keep the ranch running smoothly.

For the past four months, since the boys first came here, his life had been on hold, and it showed in the stress lines on his face when he dealt with the boys. He was muddling through parenthood, but he wasn't having any fun.

It was forty-five minutes later when she left her bedroom, freshly showered and dressed in a pair of jeans and a coral-colored tank top.

The house was quiet, but the scent of fresh brewed coffee led her through the house and to the kitchen. Jack was there, seated at the kitchen table as he stared out the window.

He didn't see her, and for a moment she simply stood in the doorway and looked at him. Once again she was struck by the sense of loneliness that clung to him. This man had once had thousands of adoring fans, but at the moment he simply looked like a man in over his head and so achingly alone.

"Good morning," she said as she walked into the room. She waved him down as he started to stand. "Just point me to the coffee cups and I can help myself."

He pointed to a nearby cabinet. "Did you sleep well?"

"Like a baby," she said as she poured herself a cup of coffee. She joined him at the table and tried to ignore the kick of pleasure she felt at the sight of him.

He was dressed in a pair of jeans and a gray T-shirt that enhanced the gunmetal hue of his eyes. His jaw was smooth-shaven, and his hair was still damp from a shower.

"What time does Betty usually get here?" she asked.

"She doesn't work on the weekends, so we're on our own for today and tomorrow. Meals are usually as easy as possible on Saturdays and Sundays."

"This morning I'd like to have breakfast alone with the boys," she said. "You can take an hour or two and go outside to chase a cow or ride the range or whatever you need to do."

"Really?" He sat back in his chair and looked at her in surprise.

She smiled. "Really." She took a sip of coffee and then continued. "Jack, you need to relax a bit. You're so tense when you're around the boys, and I think they're picking up on that. What you need to do is enjoy the process of raising them. You need to have fun with them."

He looked at her as if she were speaking a foreign language. "Fun?"

She laughed. "Remember fun, Jack?"

He smiled ruefully. "Actually, I don't remember it."

"That's what I'm going to bring back to your life, but I have to warn you things are going to get a little tough around here for the next couple days. You'd better enjoy your morning because there are going to be times you won't know who you want to strangle more—me or the kids."

He laughed. "I can't imagine that."

It was the first time she'd heard him really laugh, and the sound of his deep, rich laughter reached inside her and touched her heart. She mentally steeled herself against it, against him.

"You'd better go on before I change my mind about giving you some time off," she said with a businesslike briskness.

"You sure you don't want me to hang around and help you with breakfast for the boys?"

"I'm quite capable of taking care of it." She suddenly wanted him gone. She wanted him to take his deep, sexy voice, his clean male scent and his gorgeous robbing eyes and leave her be.

"Okay, if you insist." He got up from the table, carried his cup to the sink, then grabbed a cowboy hat from a hook near the back door. "I'll be back in a couple hours."

She nodded, and it was only when he left the house that she felt as if she could draw a deep, full breath.

There was no question that something about Jack Cortland touched her. She had never considered herself a rescuer, except when it came to the lives of children.

She had to maintain some emotional distance. She needed to focus only on her reason for being here, and that reason had nothing do with making Jack smile, bringing laughter to his lips and chasing away that cloak of loneliness that clung to him.

* * *

Jack lifted his face to the sun as he sat on the back of his horse, Domino. This was the third morning Marisa had chased him out of the house for a couple hours.

He'd been more than eager to get away this morning. He was irritated. The beautiful nanny who stirred him on a number of levels in the past two days had transformed into a mini drill sergeant barking orders.

Over the past two days she'd introduced so many new techniques his head was spinning. There was a little red chair that was a time-out place where the boys each had spent an abundance of time, and there had been times when he suspected Marisa would have liked to put *him* in that time-out chair.

She'd promised him fun, and she'd given him a rigid structure that had both he and the boys feeling downright cranky.

As he headed across the pasture, he focused his attention on the fencing, noticing several places where repair was needed.

The ranch hadn't been in great shape when Jack had returned here after his parents' deaths. He'd been back for two years, but the first year he'd done nothing but anesthetize himself with alcohol and drugs, and the ranch had fallen into more disrepair.

He waved to Sam, who was on a tractor cutting back weeds from around the barn. Then with a glance at his watch Jack realized it was time to get back to the house.

Even though he was irritated with Marisa, he couldn't help being eager to get back to the house with her and the boys. No doubt, the cute little nanny was definitely making him more than a little crazy.

He quickly brushed down Domino then put him back in his stall. Eventually he wanted to teach the boys to ride. Maybe it was time to buy a couple ponies.

He entered the house through the kitchen where Betty was working on lunch preparations. "Best thing you ever did was hire that woman," she said.

"I agree," he replied, although he'd liked Marisa better when she hadn't been riding him so hard.

"You can love them, but you also need to demand decent behavior from them. That's real love," she said.

He had just walked into the living room when the phone rang. He answered on the second ring, vaguely aware of the sound of laughter coming from the boys' bedroom.

"Jack, it's Harold."

A knot twisted in Jack's gut as he heard the sound of his ex-father-in-law's voice. "Hello, Harold."

"How are the boys?"

"Fine. They're getting along just fine," Jack replied.

"Really, that's not what I've heard."

Jack's stomach dropped to the floor. "What exactly have you heard?"

"That they have the table manners of hyenas."

Heidi. Damn, how had Harold found out about that dreadful meal? Had Heidi gone to the wealthy casino mogul man and told her tale for a price? Jack gripped the receiver more tightly against his ear.

"You don't have to worry about it, Harold," he said, pleased that his voice sounded cool and calm. "I've got a professional nanny working with them on their manners, along with some other things."

"Is she one of your bimbos from your past?"

A tide of anger swelled up inside Jack, but he stuffed it down, refusing to be baited into a screaming match with the man. Harold had never believed that Jack was faithful to Candace during their marriage. It didn't matter to Harold that his daughter probably hadn't been faithful to Jack.

"Her name is Marisa Perez. Check her out, Harold. I'm sure you'll find her credentials impeccable." At that moment Marisa and the boys came into the living room. They were all laughing and looked so happy he wanted to be a part of it. "Look, Harold, I've got to go. I'll talk to you later." He disconnected the call.

"Problems?" Marisa asked with a frown.

"I hope not," he replied, then forced a bright smile on his face. "And what has my two favorite boys laughing so hard?"

As Mick went into a long story about a bug on the floor in the bedroom, love swelled Jack's heart. He would do anything within his power to keep these boys with him.

That night he found himself alone in the living room with Marisa. The boys had gone to sleep in their beds at eight-thirty without a fuss.

"This is amazing," he said to her as he listened to the silence of the house.

She smiled. "And you were probably getting ready to fire me."

He grinned. "There have been moments in the past couple days that I thought you'd ridden me hard," he admitted. "It's taken me a while to realize that giving kids consequences for bad behavior isn't abusive."

"On the contrary, it's the most loving thing you can do for them," she replied.

All day long Jack had felt a simmering tension where she was concerned. He felt it now as he smelled the scent of her perfume, noticed how her T-shirt tugged across her full breasts.

She has a boyfriend, he reminded himself. *She's unavailable.* Still, thinking those words didn't ease the desire for her that seemed to grow stronger every day.

His irritation with her that morning seemed like an alien emotion as this afternoon he'd begun to see the results of her firm hand both with the boys and with him. By no means were things perfect yet, but they were definitely better than they had been before she'd arrived.

"I guess I should go to bed," she said.

"Don't go yet," he protested. "It's still early, and I enjoy your company."

Her cheeks turned a charming pink as she settled back into the sofa cushion. "It is early. I guess I could stay up for a little while longer." She looked at him curiously. "I might be overstepping my boundaries, but I couldn't help but hear you mention my name on the phone earlier."

A new tension twisted in Jack's stomach. "That was Harold Rothchild on the phone. Apparently he heard about a dinner that went bad just before I hired you." He quickly told her about the dinner with Heidi and the flying broccoli. When he was finished a small smile curved her lips.

"I'm sorry. I know it isn't funny," she exclaimed with her laughter barely suppressed. "But I'm just imagining that cheesy broccoli sliding down the front of her chest."

Suddenly they were both laughing with an abandon that felt wonderful. The stress of the past four months seemed to melt out of Jack.

"That felt good," he said when the laughter finally stopped.

"You need to do more of that," she replied, her brown eyes brimming with warmth.

"I haven't had anything to laugh about for a very long time," he confessed. "First there was the divorce from Candace, then my band fell apart and all the other members were ticked off at me. But the worst part was after the divorce when I wasn't getting to see the boys and I knew if I fought for custody I'd lose." He sighed heavily. "Then Candace was murdered. Now I'm struggling to pick up the pieces of my boys' lives. I still worry about losing custody."

She looked at him in surprise. "Why?"

"There's nothing Harold Rothchild would like more than to take the boys away from me—and the only way he can do that is to prove I'm an unfit father."

"Surely he couldn't do that," she replied.

Jack grimaced. "I'm not so sure. I have two strikes against me already. I'm a single man, and I don't exactly have a sterling past—and it will only take one screwup and he'll come swooping in."

"Then we can't have a screwup, right?" she replied.

She smiled, and at that moment Jack wanted nothing more than to move from his chair to the sofa and pull her into his arms. He wanted to explore exactly where that sexy scent emanated from on her body, what those lush lips tasted like in the heat of a kiss.

"Tell me about Harold Rothchild," she said, and

the question tamped down any wild desire that might have possessed Jack. "I heard he's some big casino tycoon and his family made their fortune in the diamond business."

"They owned some diamond mines in Mexico. There was a Mayan legend that one of the big diamonds that was found there held some sort of special powers. Its magic caused people to fall in love. It was made into a ring that Candace was wearing on the night of her murder."

"I read something about the ring. It was stolen that night, right? Isn't the diamond called The Tears of the Quetzal?"

Jack nodded and frowned as he thought of the man who at the moment was the bane of his existence. "Harold is working on his third wife. His first wife, June, died giving birth to Candace's youngest sister, Jenna. He and his second wife divorced, and from what I've heard the third wife is on her way out as well. Harold is powerful, and I think he hates me."

"Why would he hate you?"

"Because of my divorce from Candace. I think he believes that we split because I was sleeping around on his daughter. It doesn't seem to bother him that in all probability she was cheating on me. Maybe he thinks that if Candace and I had stayed together she wouldn't have been murdered."

"Were you in love with her?" Marisa asked.

Jack considered the question a long time before

answering. "Initially I was in lust with her. She was wild and beautiful, and we partied together for months in L.A. before we impulsively hopped a plane to Vegas and got married. Almost immediately she got pregnant with Mick. and I was ready for the partying to stop."

"But she wasn't ready to stop," Marisa said.

He nodded. "And then David came along. At the same time a couple of record producers contacted me. They told me they wanted to make me a star in my own right, turn me into a solo performer. I thought I had it all—two little boys, a gorgeous wife and a shot at becoming an artist of real standing."

His laughter held a touch of bitterness. "It wasn't until Candace and I split that I realized the record producers were more interested in her than in me. The deal fell apart, and the members of Creation were angry with me for even thinking about going out on my own. The band broke up and my marriage did the same. But I haven't answered your question, have I?"

He turned his head and stared out the window as he thought of the woman he'd married. He finally looked back at Marisa. "Did I love Candace? I loved the woman I hoped she'd become as the mother of my children, but that woman didn't exist."

"I'm sorry," Marisa said softly. "I'm sorry for you, but I'm also sorry for your boys. And now, I really should call it a night," she said and rose from the sofa.

Jack got up from his chair. "Me, too. Mornings come early with two little ones in the house."

Together they walked down the hallway, and when she got to the door of her room she turned to look at him, her gaze soft and warm. "Everything is going to be all right, Jack. You're a great father, and nobody is going to take those boys away from you."

He wasn't sure if it was her words or the fact that she looked so achingly feminine, so soft and touchable, but the desire that had simmered inside him for the past couple days returned with full force.

Almost without his volition he reached up and touched a strand of her long hair. He half expected her to jump back from him, but other than a slight flare of her eyes, she remained in place as if anticipating his next move.

He placed his hand on the back of her head and pulled her toward him until they stood breast-to-chest, hip-to-hip.

"I'm going to kiss you now," he said, unsure if it was a threat or a promise.

"I know," she replied breathlessly just before he lowered his mouth to hers.

Chapter 4

As Jack's lips claimed hers Marisa welcomed the kiss. She'd wanted this since the moment she'd met him. She'd needed to know just what his mouth would taste like pressed against hers.

Hot. It tasted hot, and as his tongue touched the tip of hers, she opened her mouth to him, allowing him to take the kiss deeper and more intimate.

In the back of her mind she knew this was wrong—that they were crossing a line that shouldn't be crossed, but she found herself helpless to stop it.

Instead she leaned into him as he wrapped his arms around her and pulled her more tightly against him. Here were the fireworks she'd missed on the

Fourth of July a week earlier, she realized as he kissed her with a mastery that weakened her knees.

It was only when he pulled her close enough and she could tell that he was aroused that her senses returned. She pushed against his chest and stepped back from him.

"That probably wasn't a good idea," she said as her heart banged rapidly in her chest.

He dropped his arms to his side. "You're right, but it was something I've wanted to do since the first moment I met you."

"Bad Jack," she said teasingly, even though she wanted nothing more than to be back in his arms. "And now it's really time for me to say good night."

She escaped into her room, her heart still beating an unsteady rhythm.

Patrick's kisses had never stirred her like this. He'd never made her feel the breathless excitement that now coursed through her veins.

For the next three days that kiss haunted her. Neither she nor Jack mentioned it again, but the memory of it was there in the air between them, snapping with energy and making things just a little bit uncomfortable.

It was mid-afternoon, and the boys were down for their naps when Jack and Marisa sat at the table in the dining room to discuss her further employment. The week of probation was over, and she had to decide if she was going to stay in his employ for the next two months.

From the kitchen the sound of a portable television played a soap opera, entertaining Betty as she began the preparations for the evening meal.

Even though Marisa's attraction to Jack made her more than a little bit nervous about continuing on here, her real concern was that she was losing all her objectivity where the boys were concerned.

She had fallen in love with Mick, who had a wonderful sense of humor and was surprisingly protective of his younger brother. And David had stolen her heart as well despite his attraction to getting through locked doors and windows.

Although they still hadn't bonded with Jack in the way she'd like to see them do, they had bonded to her, desperate for her attention and love.

She now faced Jack across the width of the dining-room table. "Our probationary week is over," she began.

"And I want you to stay until the boys are teenagers," he replied half-seriously.

She laughed and shook her head. "I can give you two months, Jack. By the end of that time the boys should be socialized enough to enter a preschool program. They need that. They need to learn to play with other children before they start school, and we need to get David out of diapers as soon as possible."

"I'll start working on that with him," Jack replied.

"You also need to understand that if I make the commitment for the two months, then I'll need my weekends off. I'd also like to take tomorrow evening off. Patrick has invited me to dinner." She needed to see the man she was supposed to be dating and was hoping that being with Patrick could banish the power of Jack's kiss from her brain.

"Why don't you invite him here for dinner?" Jack asked.

Marisa's first impulse was to say no, that she preferred to keep her work and her private life separate. But she knew that Patrick had mentioned he'd been a big fan of Jack's band, and maybe it would clear her head to see the two men together.

"That's very nice. I think he would enjoy meeting you. He told me he was once a big fan of yours," she replied.

"Good, then I'll tell Betty to make sure and set an extra plate at the table for tomorrow evening," Jack replied.

At that moment noise from the bedroom let them know the boys were awake from their naps, and with the next two months of employment arranged, Marisa got up from the table to tend to the boys.

Throughout the afternoon she reminded herself that whatever Jack felt for her was tied up in who she was professionally. She was the woman who had brought order to his chaotic existence. It was no wonder he'd kissed her. She was positive what had

prompted him to do so was a healthy dose of gratitude and nothing more.

She had to remember that. She had to remember
that Jack Cortland might make her heart race, but
she'd be a fool to fall into thinking Jack had any real
feelings for her. And Marisa had been a fool only
once in her life for a man. She wasn't about to repeat
the same mistake.

Rita Perez was frantic. She'd been frantic ever
since she'd realized the ring, Harold Rothchild's
million-dollar diamond ring, was missing.

It wasn't just a piece of expensive jewelry. It was
the ring Candace Rothchild had been wearing the
night she'd been murdered. The ring they called The
Tears of the Quetzal.

The ring not only had a Mayan legend attached
to it but it had also had a crazy past since it had come
into evidence, having been stolen from police
custody and then recovered.

And now it was gone once again.

For the hundredth time in the past week, she knelt
on the floor under her desk and searched the carpet,
even though she knew it wasn't there. The ring
hadn't accidentally fallen on the floor; it hadn't
dropped into a desk drawer. It had disappeared from
a small box that she kept locked in her gun safe.

She should never have checked it out from the
evidence room and brought it home, but she'd been

fascinated with it and had wanted to research more thoroughly how it had come to belong to the Rothchilds.

A wave of despair washed over her and made the wound on the side of her head bang with nauseating intensity. She'd probably be fired. Worse than that, if Harold found out the precious ring was missing again, he'd sue not only her but also the entire department for her negligence.

How had that ring disappeared from her gun safe? Whoever had stolen it had been a professional. They'd known just where to look and how to get in and out without her even knowing they were there.

What was she going to do? Sooner or later she was going to have to tell her superiors what had happened, and then all hell was going to break loose.

With a new burst of energy she began to pull out the desk drawers, hoping, praying that it would be found.

Once again Jack and Marisa were in the living room. It was just after nine, and David and Mick had been in bed asleep for half an hour.

"I still can't believe how easy bedtime has become," he said. "It's like a miracle."

Marisa smiled at him. "All it takes is a firm hand and consistency. That's the secret of good parenting."

"What about your mom and dad? Were they good parents?" he asked curiously.

"Absolutely." She leaned back against the corner of the sofa and drew her legs up beneath her. "Like Candace and the Rothchilds, money was never a problem in my family. My parents are quite wealthy, but they taught me values that had nothing to do with money. I started babysitting when I was about fourteen and even through college worked a variety of jobs. What about your parents?"

"They were terrific people, hardworking and possessed good old-fashioned values." A flash of pain darkened his eyes. "They taught me right, but when I got to Los Angeles and had more money than sense, all their lessons went right out the window. I think I broke their hearts."

There was nothing more appealing than a man who recognized his own frailties and regretted them, Marisa thought. "I'm sure they'd be proud of the man you've become," she said softly.

"Yeah, I'm just sorry they passed before they saw me pulling my life back together again."

"I'm sure they were confident that eventually you'd come back to the values they'd taught you as a young man," she replied.

He nodded. "You think the boys will ever call me Daddy?"

She heard the wistfulness in his voice and knew how important that was to him. "Maybe when they feel safe with you. I don't know much about their lives when they were with Candace, but from what little you've told me I would guess that most of the people who entered their lives were there only on a temporary basis. When they know you're not going anywhere and they can trust you, then maybe you won't be Jack anymore. You'll be Daddy."

He smiled at her. "What made you so smart?"

"Trust me, I'm not always smart. We all have things in our pasts that we'd prefer to forget about."

Jack raised a dark eyebrow. "Now you have me intrigued."

For just a moment she thought about sharing with him the heartache that would always be a part of her, one that had forever changed what she would expect from life.

She knew Jack would understand how foolish she'd been, that he of all people wouldn't judge her. But it felt far too intimate to share that piece of herself with him.

Once again she realized the lines were getting blurred between them. She had to remember that he was her employer and nothing more. She had to remember that she was one of those temporary people not only in the boys' lives but in Jack's as well.

She got up from the sofa. As always when it was just the two of them, she felt the need to get away, to escape from him. It was too appealing, too intimate to sit in his living room with him while night fell outside.

This whole assignment would have been easier if Jack had a wife, but of course if he had a wife Marisa probably wouldn't be here.

"Good night, Jack," she said, hoping he didn't follow her down the hallway to her room, yet in a small little place in her mind wishing he would. She wouldn't mind sharing another kiss with him, and that realization worried her.

Thankfully, he seemed to be caught up in thoughts of his own, for he murmured a good-night and remained in his chair.

Over the past couple nights they had fallen into the habit of staying up talking until around midnight or so. During those hours she'd heard a lot about the Rothchild family, and she'd told him how close she was to her aunt Rita.

Even though the conversations during those hours of the night were light and not overly personal, the end result had been a growing friendship between them. Still, it wasn't that friendship that made the most simple touch from him sizzle inside her.

She now paused in the doorway of the boys' room before going to her own. How could she not fall in love with these boys? They were children who desperately needed a mother, and she was a woman who was meant to be a mom.

With a soft smile, she went first to Mick's bedside and pulled the sheet up closer around his neck. She smoothed a strand of his blond hair off his face and pressed a kiss on his forehead. He said something incomprehensible but didn't awaken.

She moved to David's bed and tucked in one of his legs and an arm. He mumbled and smiled, as if enjoying the pleasant dreams of innocence. She kissed him, too, then moved back to the doorway.

Two months. That's all she was giving herself with them. By that time she'd have taught Jack what he needed to learn to be a good father, and the boys would have a new respect and love for him.

This was her job, to make things right for parent and child, then to walk away. But somehow she thought it was going to be more difficult than it had ever been to walk away from the boys.

And from Jack.

With a tired sigh she left the boys' bedroom and went across the hall to her own. She stepped inside, flipped on the overhead light and froze as she saw a masked man sliding open her window.

She has a boyfriend. Jack had to keep reminding himself that Marisa wasn't available to him, that she was a temporary fix in his life.

The worst mistake he had made since she'd arrived was kissing her. The memory of that single kiss had haunted him each night since. *She* haunted him, stirring inside him a want that he hadn't felt for a very long time—perhaps never before.

He was a fool. She was intelligent and had big plans for her future. She was eager to start her own agency, and the last thing she needed was to be involved with a man with his kind of past.

A scream shot him out of his chair.

Marisa! His heart leaped into his throat as he raced down the hall toward her room. She stood just inside, a hand over her mouth. When he entered she pointed to the window where the screen had been removed and the window was partially opened.

"A man. He was trying to get in," she exclaimed.

"Go check on the boys," Jack said.

"Should I call the police?" she asked.

"No." Jack barked the single word as he raced down the hallway to his bedroom. Once inside the room he pulled a lockbox from his bedroom drawer, unlocked it and withdrew his gun.

As he ran back down the hallway he glanced into the boys' room, grateful to see them both still sleeping and Marisa standing between the beds.

The hot July air wrapped around him oppressively as he left the house. He moved with stealth, keeping to the shadows of the house and trees. He was grateful for the moonlight that made his search that much easier.

When he reached the window of Marisa's bedroom he tightened his grip on the gun. The window screen was propped up against the house, but there was no sign of the intruder.

As he extended the perimeter of his search outward, a thousand questions flew through his head. Was this about Marisa? Had somebody been trying to get inside to harm her? Or was it about him?

Whoever it had been, he was apparently gone now. Jack put the screen back up in the window, then went inside.

Marisa met him in the hallway, her eyes large and still holding an edge of fear. "Nothing?" she asked.

"Nothing." He motioned her to follow him into the living room. "Whoever was out there isn't there anymore."

She curled up on the sofa, as if her fear had made her unusually cold. He set the gun on the coffee table then began to pace in front of her.

"Did you get a good look at him?" he asked.

"He had on a ski mask. Are you sure you don't want to call the police?"

"Right, I can see the headlines now. Intruder looking for drugs at Cortland Ranch. Harold Rothchild steps in to save Candace's kids." A ball of tension expanded in his chest, and for a moment he had trouble drawing a full breath.

"You think that's what it was? Somebody looking for drugs?"

He stopped pacing and looked at her. "I don't know what to think. Unless you know somebody who might want to break into your bedroom to harm you."

"I can't imagine anyone wanting to hurt me," she replied. "Surely Harold can't use it against you that there was an attempted break-in."

"You'd be surprised what he could use against me," Jack replied with an old touch of bitterness.

"Okay, if you don't want to call the police, why don't you let me call my aunt Rita? She's FBI. She can take a look around, maybe check the window for fingerprints and we can trust her not to say anything to anyone about this."

We. We can trust her. The use of the plural wasn't lost on him, and there was a certain sense of relief knowing that he wasn't in this alone.

"Would she mind coming over?" he asked.

In reply she uncurled herself and reached for the phone. Minutes later as they waited for Rita to arrive, they sat together on the sofa, and it was then that Jack decided to tell her what scared him more than anything.

"When Candace died and I was granted custody of Mick and David, Harold made a lot of threats. But the one he told me that upset me most was that it was possible that one or both of the boys might not be mine." A new surge of emotion filled his chest.

"I don't care about biology," he continued. "As far as I'm concerned both of them are mine, and I don't give a damn what a blood test would show. But one little mistake and I'm afraid Harold will order DNA tests. Then I risk losing the only thing that has given me any real meaning in my life."

She placed a hand on his arm. "Then we won't let that happen."

At that moment Rita arrived.

Jack immediately liked the no-nonsense woman who held an important role in Marisa's life. She briskly went about her work of checking for fingerprints in and around the window frame, but unfortunately there were none.

After looking around the area, she returned inside, where she sat with Jack and Marisa at the kitchen table. "If he was smart enough to wear a ski mask, then he was surely smart enough to wear gloves, hence no fingerprints," she said. She reached up and touched the bandage on the side of her head, then dropped her hand to her side.

"Maybe it was just somebody trying to get in to rob Jack," Marisa said.

"Maybe," Rita agreed. "Or I suppose it's possible it was an old fan wanting a piece of the famous Jack Cortland." She smiled at Jack, but the smile didn't last but a moment.

"What would concern me if I were you is that those two little boys of yours would be hot targets for kidnapping," she said.

Marisa gasped, and Jack sat up straighter in his chair, his blood chilling. "Everyone around these parts knows I spent most of my fortune years ago," he said.

"But not the Rothchild fortune," Rita replied. "Those boys are Harold's heirs, and everyone knows that he's probably worth more than the national debt. My recommendation would be that you beef up security around here."

An overwhelming sense of discouragement settled on Jack's shoulders as Rita stood to leave. He started to rise as well, but she waved him down. "Marisa will see me out," she said.

Jack nodded wearily as the two women left the kitchen. In the four months since he'd had the boys here with him at the ranch he'd never thought about the fact that they could be potential kidnap victims.

The idea of somebody taking his boys and using them for ransom was absolutely chilling. How did you keep children safe against an unknown threat? When there was no way to identify the face of a kidnapper? Somehow, some way he'd have to figure it out.

He forced a smile as Marisa came back into the kitchen. "Thanks for calling her."

She nodded, a worried frown creasing her forehead as she sat in the chair next to his. "She wasn't herself tonight. Something is wrong. I could feel it."

"Did you ask her about it?"

"Yes, but she assured me it was nothing, just something work related. I just hope it doesn't have anything to do with the wound on her head." She quickly told Jack about how Rita had gotten shot during the kidnapping of Jenna Rothchild.

"Yeah, I read about that in the paper," he said.

Marisa's gaze held his intently. "So what happens now?"

"I wish I knew. I guess the first order of business is to get a security system installed here. Maybe it was just somebody trying to get in to rob me," he said thoughtfully, "But it's definitely put me on notice, and I'm going to take whatever precautions I can to see that we're all safe here."

She reached across the table and gave his hand a quick squeeze, then got up. As she moved a strand of her shiny hair behind her ear, he noticed that her hand shook slightly.

Even though he knew it wasn't a good idea to try to comfort her, he got up and wrapped her in his arms.

She stood rigid for only a moment and then melted against him. He held her tight and felt the slight tremor of her body against his.

"I'm sorry you were frightened," he whispered against her ear, where he could smell that dizzying scent of her.

"It's not your fault," she replied as she buried her face into his shoulder.

"I should have had an alarm system put in here when I first moved the boys in, but nobody had ever bothered me out here and it just never entered my mind." He was rambling, wanting to keep talking, needing to continue holding her.

He'd felt alone for a very long time, but with her in his arms the loneliness no longer existed inside him.

When she finally raised her head to look at him there was no question that he was going to kiss her again. As he took her mouth with his, desire slammed through him. What he'd intended as a gentle kiss instead was hot and demanding.

She responded with a hunger that stunned him. She raised her arms and tangled her fingers in his hair as they stumbled backward and her back hit the refrigerator.

Their lips remained locked in a kiss that drove all other thoughts from his head. He slid his hands up the back of her T-shirt, wanting to feel the warmth of her bare skin against his palms.

She didn't protest but instead broke the kiss and leaned her head back, allowing him to trail his lips down the length of her neck and across her delicate collarbone.

"Marisa." He breathed her name on a sigh against her ear. "I want you. I've wanted you every day since you arrived here."

When she looked up at him he saw the flame of desire in her eyes, and that nearly shoved him over the edge. She didn't say anything but instead pulled his head back down so their lips could meet once again.

As he kissed her once again he leaned into her and slowly moved his hands from her bare back to her breasts. Her nipples pushed against the thin material of her bra, and he wanted her naked in his arms. He wanted her panting beneath him as he took her over and over again.

She moaned, a soft throaty sound that shot through him like a bolt of electricity.

He stepped back from her and took her by the hand. Neither of them said a word as he led her out of the kitchen, through the living room and down the hallway to his bedroom door.

They were just about to go into the room when Mick cried out from his bedroom. Both Jack and Marisa froze.

"Marisa," Mick cried. "I had a bad dream."

Jack dropped her hand. Whatever fire he had seen in her eyes moments ago was gone. "He needs me," she said.

Jack nodded. "Go on. I'll see you in the morning."

As she hurried back down the hallway to the boys' room two thoughts flittered through Jack's mind. Would he and Marisa ever be able to reclaim the moment that had just been lost? And would there ever come a time when his boys would cry out for him?

Chapter 5

By ten-thirty the next morning the new alarm system had been installed and Marisa prayed that these extra precautions would prevent another terrifying break-in from ever happening again.

After lunch and naps Marisa was on the floor in the living room playing with building blocks with the boys when Kent Goodall stopped by. She was grateful when the two men went outside on the front porch to visit.

Facing Jack this morning had been more difficult than she'd expected after the near intimacy of the night before.

She was grateful they hadn't followed through on

the desire that had momentarily flared out of control between them. She couldn't let herself get caught up in the heat of a moment that wouldn't last. That's what she'd done before, and she'd sworn she'd never allow it to happen again.

She was equally glad that Patrick was coming to dinner tonight. Patrick was safe. He didn't stir a craziness inside her.

She needed to see him. For the past week she and Jack had been living in a tiny bubble where it was just the two of them and the boys. She needed Patrick to bring the world in, to set her feet more firmly on the ground of reality.

"Marisa, watch!" Mick said as he built a tower of blocks higher and higher. He shoved his blond hair off his forehead with the back of his hand, a gesture Marisa had seen Jack do before.

"M'ssa, watch," David echoed and began slamming blocks one on top of the other. David's tower only got four high when the blocks tumbled to the floor. He laughed as if it were the funniest thing he'd ever seen.

As always, playing with the boys brought a wave of love into her heart. She knew from those late-evening talks with Jack that most of their early life had been spent in hotel rooms with hotel staff acting as babysitters. Then, after the divorce, Candace had shoved the boys off on nannies so they wouldn't hamper her wild lifestyle. There had been no sense of permanence and security for them from the moment they'd been born until they had come here to Jack's ranch.

They wouldn't even remember her. Within months of her leaving, the boys would forget the positive influence she'd had on their lives. It was the way it was supposed to be with professional nannies.

Still, she was surprised to realize this knowledge pained her more than a little bit. These boys had laughed and misbehaved their way right into the core of her heart like no other children had done before.

Maybe it was because on every other job she'd had in the past there had been a mother present. This was the first time Marisa had worked with a single parent.

The front door opened, and Jack stuck his head inside. "Kent and I are going to the barn. You and the boys want to come?"

Both of the boys headed for the door as Marisa pulled herself up off the floor. "Guess so," she said with a smile as the two boys barreled out the door and onto the porch.

Jack took Mick's hand and Marisa took David's. Together with Kent they all began to walk across the expanse of lawn toward the barn in the distance.

The July sun bore down on them with an oppressive heat that was searing. Marisa made a mental note to check with Jack about sunscreen for his fair little boys.

"I can already see a big change in the kids," Kent said to her. "They seem a little more calm than they were a week ago."

"That's because Jack is a little more calm," she replied with a teasing smile to Jack. "We still have a ways to go," she added.

"Still, it's nice to see them behaving better," Kent replied.

They hadn't gone far when she felt a prickly sensation in the center of her back. It was a whisper of intuition, the feeling that somebody was watching her.

She turned her head from side to side, seeking the source of the discomfort. She spied Max Burrow standing near the stables. The tall burly man leaned on a shovel, and it appeared that he was watching them…watching her.

The uneasiness increased as he met her gaze and didn't look away but rather stayed focused on them as they walked. She looked at Jack, then back toward Max, surprised to see that he had disappeared.

She mentally shook herself. Apparently the episode of the attempted break-in the night before had her more on edge than she'd thought. Surely Max hadn't been staring at her but was just resting for a moment before getting back to work.

Jack pushed open the barn door, and they all entered. Marisa caught her breath as she saw the wealth of memorabilia housed inside.

Life-size posters of the Creation band lined the walls and Jack's sparkling drum set was on a small raised platform in one corner. David released Marisa's hand and beelined to the drums.

"Welcome to Jack's past," Kent said to her. "And what a glorious past it was."

There were T-shirts and caps and CDs in glass frames. There was also a glassed-in room that Marisa assumed was the recording studio. "This stuff must be worth a fortune," she exclaimed.

"Yeah, Jack had it all after he left us poor folks behind for the big-time," Kent replied. He clapped a hand on Jack's back. "But we're glad to have him back here where he belongs."

David hit the cymbals and laughed with glee.

"David, I don't think you're supposed to touch that," Marisa exclaimed.

"He's all right," Jack replied with an easy smile. "He can't hurt anything."

"Maybe he's the next generation of drumming talent," Kent said.

"God, I hope not," Jack replied fervently. "I'd much rather see the boys go to college than join a band."

Mick had found a set of dolls fashioned after the band members and sat on the floor with them. "No wonder the boys like to come out here," Marisa said. "It's like a big wonderland." She winced as David banged on the snare drum.

Jack smiled and then touched Kent on the arm. "Come on, I'll get you that music you wanted."

As Jack and Kent went into the recording studio area, Marisa looked more closely at the posters on the walls.

Although his hair had been much longer and there had been a wildness in his eyes that was no longer present, Jack had still been one hot hunk when he'd been in his band.

She stopped in front of one particular photo and stared at him. He was standing at his drums, his sweaty T-shirt plastered against his broad chest and oh my…what a chest it was.

The memory of the kiss, the caresses they'd shared jumped unbidden into her head, and her body temperature rose at least ten degrees.

She whirled around as the two men came back out of the recording studio, Kent clutching several sheets of music in his hand.

"Thanks," he said to Jack. "I really appreciate it."

Jack shrugged. "I'm never going to do anything with it. Your band might as well use it." He smiled at Marisa. "We're done in here. Mick, David, come on. We're going back to the house."

David banged the cymbal once again as Mick put the dolls back on the stands where they belonged. David eyed his father with more than a hint of mutiny.

Marisa moved closer to Jack. "Give him a reason to do as you asked," she said softly.

"The time-out chair?" he asked below his breath.

Marisa smiled. "Why don't you try something positive?"

Jack frowned, and she tried not to notice that wonderfully clean male scent of him, desperately tried to forget how his hands had felt so hot and needy on her bare skin.

"Hey, buddy, let's go back to the house and we'll get out the trucks and make a road through the living room," Jack said.

David looked at him thoughtfully, then with a happy grin left the drums and approached Jack. Jack picked him up in his arms, and Marisa's heart expanded. Jack was learning and proving to be quite an amazing daddy.

"And we can make bumps in the road with pillows," Mick said eagerly as they all headed back to the house.

"Yeah, bumps!" David echoed.

Kent headed for his car and waved goodbye.

"You gave him music?" she asked Jack.

"A couple of songs I wrote a long time ago. I wasn't going to do anything with them, and Kent had some interest in using them with his band," he replied.

"That was a nice thing for you to do," she said.

He shrugged. "Kent's been a good friend over the years. It's really no big deal."

They entered the house, and for the next hour Jack sat on the living-room floor playing with his sons.

He's good with them, Marisa thought as she watched their play. He was patient and had a sense of make-believe that they responded to with glee.

As far as Marisa was concerned there was nothing more appealing than a man who could get in touch with the boy inside of him for the sake of his small sons. It didn't take long for the truck game to evolve into a wrestling match.

Marisa laughed as the two boys piled on top of Jack, screaming and giggling with abandon. It was the first time she'd seen the three of them just having fun together.

"Get M'ssa," David yelled, his bright blue eyes sparkling with excitement.

Suddenly it wasn't just the three of them on the floor in a pile but it was her as well. Jack had her on her back and tickled her ribs as the boys squealed with delight and danced around them.

"Stop, please," she cried amid bursts of laughter. He stopped, and for just a minute he remained on top of her, staring down at her.

There was no laughter in his eyes; rather there was a hot flash of fire that left her breathless in a way the tickling had not.

Instantly he stood and held out a hand to help her up off the floor. "Thanks," she murmured as she got to her feet. She didn't look at him as a blush warmed her cheeks. "Okay, boys, it's time to pick up the toys," she said.

"I'll see to the cleanup," Jack said, his voice deeper than usual. "I'm sure you'd like some time to shower and get ready for dinner."

Dinner with Patrick. She looked at her watch and realized dinner was less than an hour away. "Thanks, I appreciate it."

As she walked down the hallway to her bedroom, she tried to ignore the ball of heat that still burned in her stomach, a flame that had been ignited by the desire in Jack's eyes.

He'd confessed to her one night when the boys had been in bed that he hadn't been with any woman since his divorce from Candace. That was a long time for a man to go without a woman.

Surely it was nothing more than close proximity that had him looking at her as if she were his favorite dessert.

The worst thing she could do was allow herself to get caught up in the family atmosphere, in the intimacy of this particular assignment.

Jack was dangerous to her. She felt it in her heart, in her soul. The look in his eyes, the heat of his touch reminded her of that time in her life when she'd risked everything—and lost.

Jack didn't like him. It took him about fifteen minutes for him to make the judgment call that Patrick Moore was arrogant, abrasive and far too smooth.

He especially didn't like the way the man looked at Marisa—with a possessiveness that rankled Jack.

"It's a shame your band broke up," Patrick said as he helped himself to more of Betty's mashed potatoes. "But I guess that wild lifestyle really took a toll on you."

It was as if he wanted to remind Marisa that Jack was an old has-been with a questionable past. "It was time for me to move on to a new phase in my life," Jack replied easily. "I had more important things to do than make music." He looked pointedly at his sons, who so far had behaved admirably through the meal.

"Yeah, but I heard the transition from rock star to family man has been pretty tough for you. Didn't you have a stint in rehab?"

"Patrick!" Marisa let out a short uncomfortable laugh, and then gave him a look of disapproval.

"I'm just asking," he said with a look of innocence.

"It's all right," Jack said to Marisa, then turned his attention back to Patrick. "Actually, no. I never spent any time in rehab, and I'm too busy raising kids now to even think about drugs or alcohol."

"I didn't mean to offend you in any way," Patrick said hurriedly.

"No offense taken," Jack replied smoothly, although he found everything about Patrick offensive. His hair was too dark, too neat. His dress shirt didn't have a single wrinkle and he possessed a cool facade that annoyed Jack.

Marisa deserved a man with more passion, one who had a lust for life burning inside him. She deserved somebody like Jack. He mentally shook himself at this silly thought.

He conceded that his feelings for Patrick were colored by his growing desire for Marisa. He told himself he had no right to judge the kind of man Marisa dated.

Marisa was his employee, and in two months' time she'd be gone from his life. He needed to gain some distance from his lovely nanny.

Perhaps someday there would be a woman who would fit neatly into his life, but it wasn't going to be Marisa and it wasn't going to happen for a long time. David and Mick were all that were important to him, and what he wanted more than anything else on this earth was for them to trust him enough to call him Daddy.

The rest of the meal passed with pleasant, easy conversation, and when they were finished eating Jack took the boys into their bedroom to give Marisa and her boyfriend some time alone.

At seven-thirty he gave the boys their baths and got them into their pajamas. Once they had fallen asleep he remained in the room, seated between their two beds.

His mind raced back to the night before and what Rita Perez had told him. He'd never thought about his sons being likely candidates for kidnapping.

He'd been so busy just trying to get through each day with them he hadn't thought of the bigger ramifications of them living here with him.

There was no question that as Harold's grandkids, the boys would be worth a fortune to a potential kidnapper.

Was the man who had tried to break in simply a robber looking for a quick score of cash or drugs? Why break into a house where people were not only home but were still awake?

He frowned thoughtfully. If the intruder had watched the house for any length of time he might have known that it was habit for Marisa and Jack to stay up late talking in the living room. Perhaps he meant to use that time to get in, maybe steal whatever he could find in Jack's room, then get out before he and Marisa headed off to bed.

Or had he attempted to get in to somehow grab the boys? Had there been an accomplice standing outside the boys' bedroom window, waiting for sleeping kids to be handed to him? A rush of cold air blew through Jack at the very thought.

It was all assumption, but it was the kind of speculation that could keep a man awake at night.

He didn't know how long he'd been sitting there when the phone rang. He left the boys' room and went down the hallway to his bedroom, where he grabbed the receiver next to the bed.

"Jack, it's Harold."

Jack barely stifled his groan. "Hello, Harold. What's up?"

"Why didn't you tell me? I heard somebody tried to break into your house last night."

Jack stiffened. "How did you hear about that?"

"That isn't important. What's important is the safety of those boys. If you can't keep your home safe, then maybe it's time I step in."

"That isn't necessary," Jack exclaimed, his blood rushing to his brain in a burst of anger. "I've got it covered. In fact, I had a state-of-the-art security system installed this morning. I have it all under control, Harold. There's nothing for you to worry about."

"You're on notice, Jack. Keep in mind that it's very possible you have no real legal claim to the boys. If I hear any more news about potential threats to them, then I'll have them yanked out of your custody so fast your head will spin. And you know I have the power to do that."

"I'm well aware of what you're capable of," Jack replied dryly. "Like I said, everything is under control here. There's no reason for you to worry."

Jack slammed down the receiver, his stomach burning with frustrated rage. He hated the fact that Harold had managed to remind him that one or both of the boys might not be his.

"It's very possible you have no real legal claim to those boys." Harold's words whirled in Jack's head, making him feel ill. He'd like to think that

Harold wouldn't go there to get the boys, that he would be reluctant to paint Candace as a woman who didn't know who the father of her children had been.

But he knew that Harold was ruthless enough to do such a thing to get what he wanted. Candace's reputation wasn't exactly stellar to begin with, and if Harold decided he wanted custody of the boys then he'd do whatever necessary to get it.

He leaned his head back and listened to the sound of the boys' breathing. He felt like he'd already missed so many moments of their lives. He couldn't imagine them being ripped away from him now.

Who was feeding Harold this information? Did he have somebody watching the house? Or was somebody in his house sharing private info with the man?

He left the bedroom, and as he walked back into the living room Marisa came in the front door, apparently having walked Patrick out to his car to tell him goodbye.

"Thank you for this evening," she said and then frowned. "What's wrong?"

"Harold just called. He'd heard about the attempted break-in last night."

She sucked in a breath. "How?"

"I don't know, but I intend to find out." He motioned her to follow him into the kitchen, where he noticed she'd cleaned up all remnants of the evening meal.

They sat at the table, and he stared at her, his mind whirling at a frantic pace. "Somebody is feeding Harold information. When he heard about the dinner date gone bad I just assumed Heidi had somehow made contact with him. But this puts a whole new spin on things."

"Rita didn't know about your dinner date, and in any case she would never betray my trust," Marisa said quickly.

Jack nodded. "Then that leaves Kent, Sam, Max or Betty. And of course you," he added.

A stain of color crept into her cheeks, letting him know he'd made her angry. "If you really think I'm capable of such duplicity then you need to fire me right now," she exclaimed.

"I'm not saying you're responsible," he protested. "Marisa, think about it, I'd be a fool not to consider everyone right now." He sighed in frustration. "It appears that somebody I trust, somebody who is in my confidence, is betraying me."

Some of the color in her cheeks faded. "I know you have no reason to trust me, but it isn't me, Jack. I don't know Harold Rothchild. I've never spoken to the man in my life. I certainly want what's in the best interest of Mick and David, and I've told you that as far as I'm concerned that's having them here with you."

"I trust you, Marisa," he said, and as the words left his mouth he recognized the truth in them. Even though he'd only known her a little over a week, he trusted her without a doubt. "What I have to figure out is who is betraying me." He rubbed a hand wearily across his forehead. "Somebody is playing with my life, Marisa."

It had been a long time since Jack's anger had been directed outward instead of inward. But now a wave of anger bigger than any he'd ever known filled him. "More important, somebody is playing with my boys' lives, and when I find out who it is, I'll make them damned sorry they ever did."

Chapter 6

"I've invited Kent to have breakfast with us," Jack said first thing the next morning.

Marisa took a sip of her coffee and eyed him over the rim of her cup. He didn't look particularly friendly. A knot of tension throbbed in his jaw, and his eyes were stormy.

"You don't look too happy at the prospect of a guest for breakfast," she observed.

"I lay awake half the night thinking about who might be selling me out to Harold," he replied. He shoved his empty coffee cup aside and stared out the dining-room window, where despite the early hour the Nevada sun already looked blazing hot.

"What about Betty?" she asked softly, hoping the woman working in the kitchen wouldn't hear her. "Or maybe Sam or Max?"

Jack turned back to look at her. "I just can't imagine it. She's more interested in soap operas and talk shows than in what's going on in this house. As far as Sam and Max are concerned, I'm not even sure they knew what happened during my dinner with Heidi. That leaves Kent."

It was obvious by the expression on his face that the idea that his friend was capable of such a thing hurt him. "Maybe there's another answer. Maybe Harold has somebody watching the house," she offered.

She thought of those moments outside the day before when she'd thought somebody was watching her. Maybe it hadn't been Max's gaze that she'd felt on her. Maybe somebody else had been hiding nearby, watching her, watching them all.

"Maybe," Jack replied, but he didn't sound convinced. "I'll know by the time breakfast is over if Kent is really my friend or not." He shoved back from the table and stood. "He's always been a terrible liar. I'm going to head outside for a little while. I'll be back soon."

She watched him go and once again had the impression of a lonely man who wasn't sure who he could trust in his life.

What must it be like to have two precious

children and be afraid all the time that some powerful entity might steal them away?

She frowned thoughtfully and stared at his coffee mug. Did she dare? She knew what she was contemplating would far exceed the boundaries of her position, but nevertheless she grabbed Jack's coffee cup and carried it to her bedroom. A few moments later she then returned to the kitchen and asked Betty for a small paper bag.

Betty gave her the bag, then looked pointedly at the door, as if inviting Marisa to leave. But instead Marisa sat at the table and eyed the woman who had been working for Jack since the boys had come to stay.

"You enjoy cooking?" she asked, even though she knew it was a foolish question.

"It's what I know how to do," Betty replied.

"What made you decide to come and work for Jack?"

Betty stirred a simmering skillet full of hash browns then wiped her hands on a towel and turned back to face Marisa. "I was a good friend of Jack's mother. A fine woman, she was. When Jack put out the word that he needed some household help there weren't many people lining up for the jobs." She shrugged. "You know his reputation wasn't the best. But I knew Jack's mother would want those boys to eat well so I decided to come to work for him."

"And you like working for him?"

"The pay is good, between meals I get to watch my television shows and I'm in my own house by six every night. What's not to like?"

"Your husband doesn't mind you being here every day?" Marisa asked.

"My Joe left me a year ago. Dropped dead of a heart attack at a slot machine in downtown Vegas. We never had any kids." She sighed. "I knew early on that I wasn't one of those maternal types. This job fills in the long hours of the days."

"I know Jack appreciates you being here for him," Marisa said as she got up from the table. She wasn't sure what she'd hoped to accomplish, but like Jack she couldn't imagine this woman being the pipeline of information to Harold Rothchild.

She was about to walk out of the kitchen when Betty called her name. She turned back to face the old woman.

"That woman Jack married broke his heart. I hope you don't plan on doing the same thing."

Marisa stared at the older woman in stunned surprise. "I'm an employee, just like you," she replied.

Betty snorted and turned back to the stove.

Marisa hurried to her bedroom, where she tucked Jack's coffee cup into the paper bag. Then noise from the boys' bedroom let her know they were awake, and she hurried into their room to help them dress for the day.

It was eight o'clock when Kent arrived and they all sat down for breakfast. The conversation remained pleasant throughout the meal although Marisa could feel tension wafting off Jack. Kent seemed oblivious to the stress that tightened Jack's jaw and filled the air as the meal came to an end.

"I'll just take the boys to their room to play," Marisa said as she rose from the table.

"Why don't you let them play on their own? I'd like you to stay here," Jack replied.

She really didn't want to be a part of the confrontation she knew was coming, but she also didn't want to leave if Jack needed her to stay. She got the boys out of their booster seats, told them to play in their room and then returned to her chair at the table.

"What's up?" Kent asked as if for the first time feeling the tension that rode thick in the air. He looked at Marisa and then back at Jack.

"We've been good friends for a long time, haven't we, Kent?" Jack asked, his voice deceptively calm.

"Except for your Los Angeles years, sure. Best friends," Kent replied. Once again he shot a quick glance at Marisa, then looked back at Jack and shifted uncomfortably in his chair. "What's going on?"

"You've been a great friend to me, but I know you and your band have been struggling. I imagine money is tight," Jack said.

"Money's always tight," Kent said with a small humorless laugh. "There's nothing new about that, but I always get by."

"I've got a problem, Kent."

"What's that?" Kent gazed at him warily.

"Somebody close to me is feeding Harold Rothchild information about the boys." It was obvious from Jack's tone that this was difficult for him.

Kent sat back in his chair and stared at Jack. "Are you accusing me? You really think I'd do something like that?" His face reddened. "You invite me here for breakfast and then accuse me of something like that? You're crazy, man."

"Kent, I'm not accusing," Jack protested. "I'm just asking."

Kent scooted his chair back from the table and stood. "I can't believe you'd think I'd do something like that to you. You're my closest friend."

He slammed his hands down on the table and glared at Jack. "If I were you, I'd look a little closer to home." He looked pointedly at Marisa and then at Jack. "Remember Ramona? The showgirl who is friends with Marisa? Guess where she works, Jack. At Rothchild's casino. You want to find a snake? Beat the grass in your house, Jack."

Marisa gasped as Kent stalked out of the kitchen and a moment later the front door slammed shut with a resounding bang.

Jack reached for his glass of water and Marisa

couldn't help but notice that his hand trembled slightly. "That went well," he said dryly.

"Did you believe him?" she asked softly.

"I don't know what to believe." His eyes looked hollow and dark. "I just know I feel like I'm on borrowed time with the boys, and I don't know how to change that."

Mick came into the dining room. "David went out the window," he said. "He wanted to play the drums again."

Both Marisa and Jack jumped up from the table and raced for the front door.

"I thought these locks on the windows were child-proof," Marisa exclaimed.

"Apparently they aren't David-proof," Jack replied.

As Jack raced after the little boy who was halfway to the barn, Marisa stood on the porch and wondered how on earth this father was going to fight somebody as wealthy and as powerful as Harold Rothchild?

Jack wandered the living room long after the boys had gone to bed. Marisa had helped him get them settled in for the night then she had left to go visit her aunt Rita.

He was surprised by how much he felt her absence. It was as if she'd taken some of the energy in the house with her when she'd gone.

The fight with Kent that morning had left a bad taste in his mouth that had lingered throughout the day. Jack had never been the kind of man who looked for a confrontation. Nothing had ever been important enough for him to fight over until now. For Mick and David he'd confront a five-headed monster.

He went into the kitchen and decided to put on a short pot of coffee. He was reluctant to call it a night and go to bed until Marisa got home safe and sound.

It was funny how quickly she'd become a part of his routine. He liked the time they spent visiting after the boys had gone to bed. He enjoyed the sound of her laughter, a rich, joyous sound that never failed to make him smile.

It wasn't just the loving way she interacted with the boys that drew him to her. She seemed to know instinctively when to give him space and when to ride him hard.

He liked the way her hair sparkled in the light, how the scent of her flooded his senses.

In fact, there was nothing about Marisa Perez he didn't like.

After the coffee had brewed he poured himself a cup and sat at the table. He rarely sat in the kitchen, had come to consider the room strictly Betty's territory.

It was a nice, warm room, and he had many memories of meals at this very table with his mother and father. Many nights Kent had joined them, and Jack's mom had often joked that she must have been asleep when they'd adopted Kent.

He wrapped his hands around the warm coffee mug as he thought of Kent. Betrayal was always tough to take but particularly so when it came at the hands of a friend.

He was still sitting at the table at ten-thirty when he heard the front door open and the beep of the security alarm preparing to ring. The beeping lasted only a minute then stopped as the code was entered.

He smelled her before she entered the room, that slightly spicy floral that heated his blood and left him wanting more.

"Hi," she said. "I wasn't sure you'd still be up."

"I decided to make some coffee. There's a cup still there if you want it."

"No, thanks. Too late for caffeine for me." She sat in the chair across from him at the table. "Everything all right here?"

"Fine. I managed to fix the lock on the window where David escaped earlier today. If I ever have trouble opening a bottle of aspirin I'm giving the bottle to him."

Marisa laughed. "We're just going to have to be vigilant about keeping the alarm on not just at night but also during the day. That way we'll know when he manages to get a window or a door open."

"I don't understand why he keeps trying to get

out. Today he wasn't even running toward the barn. He was just running."

"Curiosity," she replied. "David is curious about everything. When he starts school he's probably going to challenge his teachers."

"I have a feeling he's going to challenge me. How was your visit with your aunt? Everything okay?"

She frowned. "I still get the feeling that something's wrong, that she's worried about something, but I can't get her to confide in me. She says it's work related and that's all she would tell me. You know she's been working on Candace's murder case."

"Maybe they finally have some leads to the killer," he replied. "It would be nice to see justice done and the guilty behind bars. I think maybe that would give Harold some peace."

"Have you heard any more from him? Any more phone calls tonight?"

Jack shook his head. "No, but I realize it's just a matter of time." A new wave of discouragement filled him. His heart felt as if it weighed about a hundred pounds.

"What made you decide to get clean and sober, Jack?" she asked.

He leaned back in his chair, surprised by the question. But he realized that in all the conversations they'd shared, they'd never talk about this particular part of his past.

"Candace and I were big on the party scene." He frowned thoughtfully. "It was what brought us together, and for a long time I think it was what kept us together. The only time we stopped was when she was pregnant with the boys."

He stared out the nearby window, thinking about those days with Candace. Many of the early days of their marriage were nothing more than a blur. They had rarely been sober back then.

He turned his attention back to Marisa. "It was after David was born that I tried to change our life. I wanted to be the kind of father the boys needed, and that meant no more booze and no more drugs." He sighed. "Ultimately I think that's why Candace divorced me—because I wasn't fun anymore."

"She wasn't ready to give up the fun?"

A dry laugh escaped him. "I'm not sure what it would have taken for Candace to turn her life around, but it wasn't me or the boys. So we divorced and she took the boys. She made it almost impossible for me to have any interaction with them. She took them to Europe for several months, then back to Los Angeles. She was rarely in one place for long."

"And so you came back here," Marisa said.

He nodded. "And proceeded to drink myself into a stupor. For the next six months I pretty much stayed drunk. It was Kent who came over to see that I ate, to check on me to make sure I was still alive." He grimaced. "It's a time in my life I'm not proud of."

"So what turned things around for you?"

"One morning I stumbled into the bathroom and stared at myself in the mirror. I looked dead. I looked like all I was waiting for was somebody to shovel dirt over me." He met her gaze. "On the sink in my master bath is a small photo of my parents. I stared at that picture and was ashamed of who I was, of what I'd become."

He thought of that single defining moment. It was as if his parents had reached out to him from their graves.

"I also realized at that moment that it was possible at some point in the future the boys might need me. I knew eventually I'd have to justify the choices I'd made in my life to them." His voice deepened. "I didn't know if it would be five years or fifteen, but some day those boys would want to get to know me and that got me clean and sober. Being a drunk wasn't something I wanted to have to explain."

Marisa stared at him for a long moment, then turned her head to look out the window, her brow furrowed in thought.

Jack tried not to notice the soft curve of her jaw line, how the yellow tank top she wore clung to her full breasts. His head filled with the memory of how those breasts had felt in his hands, how her mouth had clung to his as if they were both drowning.

He felt himself getting aroused at the very thought and chastised himself for letting his mind wander.

Needing to do something—anything—to cleanse the erotic images from his head, he got up from the table, poured himself another cup of coffee and stood with his hips against the counter. At least with this distance between them he couldn't smell her fragrance.

She finally looked at him, her gaze as somber as he'd ever seen it. "You told me that you have two strikes against you if push comes to shove over custody of the boys. The first was your past."

He nodded slowly, unsure where she was going with this.

"But you've never been arrested, and most of the stories of your legendary partying were in the tabloids, right?"

"Right," he agreed.

"Which are not always true."

"Definitely," he said dryly. "The tabloid reports were always full of untruths and exaggerations."

"You've kept a very low profile since moving back here to the ranch, and nobody can make a case that you aren't an upstanding citizen now."

He moved back to the table and sat, still unable to guess where she was going with all this. "I suppose that's right."

"So really the only issue is the fact that you're a

single man trying to raise two children alone. We could fix that. We could make sure that Harold couldn't use that fact against you."

"And how would we do that?" he asked.

She held his gaze intently. "You could marry me."

Chapter 7

Marisa saw shock take possession of his features. His eyes widened and his mouth fell open, and she took advantage of his momentary speechlessness.

"Think about it, Jack. It would be a strictly business relationship," she continued. "Everything would stay just as it is now, including our sleeping arrangements." She hoped the blush she felt inside didn't show on her cheeks. "The only difference would be the picture we present outside this house—as a happily married couple raising the boys in a two-parent home."

"That's a crazy idea," he said, but she couldn't help but see the hope that leaped into his eyes. "Isn't it?" he added.

"There's absolutely nothing questionable in my past, and raising children has been my job. No judge could look at me and the way I have lived my life so far and deem me unacceptable as a stepmother to the boys."

"But why would you want to do that?" He narrowed his eyes slightly. "What's in it for you, Marisa?"

"I'll get to raise Mick and David. Jack, I've fallen in love with your boys. I care about them. After all they've been through, they need a stable life, and I can help provide that for them. I wouldn't just be doing this for you but I'd be doing it for myself as well."

"But what about Patrick?"

"I told you that we were just casually dating. It's nothing serious," she replied.

"He didn't look like it was just casual for him." Jack took a sip of his coffee, his gaze not leaving hers over the rim of his mug.

"That doesn't matter. This is my choice, Jack." She'd thought about it all night and throughout the day. There was a part of her that knew it was an insane idea, but there was a bigger part of her that somehow felt it was right.

He lowered his cup to the table. "Marisa, you're bright and you're beautiful. Why would you want to get yourself involved in this kind of a relationship? Why not marry some man and raise kids of your own?"

Her heart squeezed painfully at the question. She looked down at the top of the table, unable to look at him as she revisited the most painful time in her past.

"I was a junior in college when I met a guy named Tom, and we started a wild, passionate relationship." Her throat grew dry as she thought of those nights with Tom—not because of any residual desire but rather because she'd been such a fool.

"I was crazy about him, and I thought he was crazy about me. I didn't realize I was nothing more than a booty call for him." This time she felt the heat that filled her cheeks. "I found out just how little I meant to him when I discovered I was pregnant and he told me I was on my own."

Jack's only response was a tightening of his jaw. "It was okay," she hurriedly added. "Even though the pregnancy was unplanned and Tom had disappeared, I was thrilled to be pregnant, and I wanted the baby desperately."

The knot of pain in her chest expanded, squeezing out the breath in her lungs. "I didn't tell my parents. I didn't tell anyone about my condition except Aunt Rita. I was going to tell my parents once I had it figured out how to continue college and be a single parent." A lump rose to her throat. "To be honest, I was afraid they'd try to talk me into getting an abortion, and that was something I'd never consider."

She halted, unable to go on for a moment as her

heart shattered all over again. Tears burned in her eyes, but she refused to allow them to fall. She'd cried enough tears to fill the ocean when she'd been going through the trauma.

Jack reached across the table and took one of her hands in his. He said nothing but waited for her to gain her composure.

The warmth of his hand, big and strong around hers, helped and she drew a deep, tremulous breath. "I was just beginning my sixth month when I started to bleed and then miscarried. I was devastated, but even more devastating than that was when the doctor told me in order to save my life they had to do a complete hysterectomy."

"God, Marisa, I'm sorry. I'm so sorry for you," he said. His features were filled with compassion.

She pulled her hand from his and instead wrapped her arms around herself. "Thanks, but now surely you understand why I'm willing to do this. I'm never going to have my own babies, Jack. I'm never going to have a family of my own." She swallowed hard. "So if you agree to this business arrangement we erase one of the strikes against you and I get to be a mommy to Mick and David."

She knew what she was proposing sounded impulsive, especially given the short time she'd known Jack and the boys. But she couldn't help but follow her heart, and her heart was telling her that this was where she belonged…at least for now.

He shoved a strand of his dark hair off his forehead with the back of his hand. "I need to think about this," he finally said. "I mean, this is all happening so fast."

"Of course," she agreed. She immediately got up from the table. "I'm going to bed. I'll see you in the morning."

She left him seated at the table, staring out the window into the dark of night. She had no idea if he'd agree to her plan or not. It was out of her hands.

As she got ready for bed she thought of the offer she'd just made to Jack. She wasn't sure when it had first blossomed in her head, but the moment it had she'd embraced it.

It made a crazy kind of sense. She could live in a loveless, passionless marriage if the payoff was being able to raise Mick and David. What she didn't know was if Jack was willing to make the same kind of sacrifice.

There was no question that there was a smoldering desire between her and Jack, but she wouldn't complicate matters by diving headfirst into something wild and hot and dangerous.

She fell asleep almost immediately and dreamed of Jack. In her dreams they were making love, and she awakened the next morning feeling restless and edgy.

After showering and dressing for the day, she remained in her room until it was late enough for her to call Patrick. Whether Jack agreed to her plan or not, she'd decided to call it quits with the handsome accountant.

She'd been comfortable dating Patrick because he didn't inspire great passion in her. Jack inspired passion, but she didn't intend to follow through on it. She was putting her heart far more at risk by offering to be Jack's wife, but as she thought of the two precious boys, she thought the risk was worth it.

Besides, it wasn't really fair to continue seeing Patrick knowing that they had no future together. Eventually Patrick would want to get married and have children, and that was something she would never be able to give him. It was time to cut him loose so he could find the woman who would be his future.

He answered his phone on the second ring, obviously identifying her cell phone number from caller ID.

"What a pleasant surprise," he exclaimed. "I was just getting ready for work and thinking about you."

"I've been thinking about you, too," she replied. She hated the fact that she was going to hurt him. But better to hurt him now in the early stages of their relationship than later.

"Patrick, you're a wonderful man and someday you're going to make some woman very happy," she began.

"Why do I get the feeling this call is a kiss-off?"

Marisa sighed. "Because I guess it is. Patrick, I've enjoyed the time I've spent with you, but I'm not in a place in my life right now to want a relationship. I'm focused on my work here and two little boys who need me."

"Have I done something to offend you?" he asked quietly.

"No, not at all," she hurriedly replied. "This is about me, Patrick, not about you. I just think it would be better if we stopped seeing one another."

"You know that's not what I want," he replied in a husky voice. "But I can't do anything but respect your decision. You know where to find me if you ever need anything."

"I do—and thanks." She was grateful it hadn't gotten messy and was rather surprised that it had been so easy. She hung up and went into the dining room, where Jack was already seated at the table.

"Good morning," she said and tried not to notice how handsome he looked in a short-sleeved blue shirt and his worn jeans.

The aroma of frying bacon came from the kitchen along with the faint noise of the small television.

Marisa sat next to him and a wave of heat shot through her as she caught the scent of shaving cream and minty soap that wafted from him. Yes, she felt desire for Jack, but she reminded herself that it was an emotion that caused more grief than pleasure.

"Did you sleep well?" he asked.

"Like a baby."

"Change your mind about what you proposed to me?"

She studied his features, trying to discern what he was thinking, but his face was schooled into an enigmatic mask that made it impossible to see into his mind. "No, I still think it's a viable plan."

At that moment she heard the sound of childish laughter and knew the boys were awake. "I'll be right back," she said.

It took her only minutes to wash and dress Mick and David and then get them buckled into their booster seats at the table.

By that time Betty had served breakfast and they all began to eat. Jack ate for a few minutes in silence, then put his fork down and looked at her once again.

"What happens if we go through with it and Harold manages to get custody of the boys anyway?" he asked.

"Then we divorce," she replied. "Quick and easy—no harm, no foul." She'd once held the idea that when she married it would be forever, that she would be with the man she chose to exchange vows with for the rest of her natural life. But fate had changed her expectations.

"You know we're both more than a little bit crazy to even be contemplating this." His gray eyes studied her thoughtfully. "I'm still not sure why you'd be willing to do this for me."

"I'm not doing it for you. I'm doing it for Mick and David, and I'm doing it for me," she replied. The last thing she wanted was for Jack to know that there was a small piece of her heart that belonged just a little bit to him. She didn't even want to access that place herself.

Strictly business, she told herself even as the thought of Jack's lips against hers created a small ball of warmth in the pit of her stomach.

"You have anything special planned for this afternoon?" he asked.

Her heart seemed to skip a beat. "Nothing out of the ordinary."

"Then why don't we get dressed up and head down to the license office, then visit one of the tacky wedding chapels Las Vegas has to offer?"

Now was the time for her to change her mind, she thought. Maybe it was crazy; perhaps she hadn't considered all the ramifications.

"M'ssa, look!" David said. He grinned at her as he balanced a piece of round oat cereal on the end of his nose.

"Marisa, look, I can do it, too," Mick said and dug into his cereal bowl.

As always, her heart filled her chest at their antics. Yes, this whole scheme was probably crazy, and she was positive she hadn't completely thought it all through. But she turned to Jack and smiled.

"Just tell me what time to be ready," she said,

knowing that she had just made a decision that would forever change her life. It could be a wonderfully positive change or it could leave her utterly desolate for the second time in her life.

Harold Rothchild had many things that he regretted about his life. At the moment there was only one regret on his mind as he gazed at the gorgeous blond trophy wife seated opposite him at the long mahogany dining room table.

He'd found her incredibly sexy when he'd initially met her and truth be told she'd stroked his ego by appearing to be crazy about him. They hadn't been seeing each other for long when she'd told him she thought she was pregnant. Impulsively he'd married her and regretted it ever since.

The pregnancy had yielded a son who was now five years old. Unfortunately the bloom had definitely worn off the marriage.

It hadn't taken Harold long to be bored—bored to tears with his young wife who could only have meaningful discussions about who had worn what to which charity function and what designer was having a tremendous sale.

It was enough to make a man think fondly of the wife he'd divorced. Anna had been a good wife and had tried to be a good mother to the three girls he'd brought into the marriage. And he'd come to love Anna's daughter, Silver, as if she were his own.

Lately he'd been thinking more and more about his second wife.

He focused his attention back on the financial section of the morning newspaper.

No matter how bad the economy got, people still loved to gamble. Business had never been better at the casino as people blew their money on the chance of hitting it big.

Still, he found his concentration wandering from finances to family matters. He wondered if things would have been different for Candace if his first wife, June, hadn't died.

Candace had been a handful from the moment of her birth. Wild and impetuous, beautiful and troubled, but Harold would always believe that the reason for her murder had been that damned diamond ring.

The Tears of the Quetzal, so named for the resplendent Quetzal bird of Mexico. Like the bird, the diamond had possessed magnificent colors of golds and greens and deeper hues of blue and violet. His stomach muscles clenched with tension as he thought of the diamond.

It had been found in one of his father's diamond mines, and Harold would never forget that day—it was burned into his head and occasionally gave him nightmares that awakened him in the middle of the night.

He knew the legend attached to the ring, that it

had special powers and would bring love to anyone who came into contact with it.

It was a charming little legend, but Harold knew the truth. He knew that until the ring was back in his possession, it had the potential to wreak havoc on his family. Candace's murder had only been the first of a string of tragedies waiting to happen.

Only Harold knew the true story, that from the moment the diamond had been found it had been bathed in blood. And he got up every morning and went to bed every night terrified by what might happen next.

Chapter 8

The chapel was gaudy, like so much of what Las Vegas had to offer. Jack suddenly wished he had picked another place to exchange vows with Marisa. She deserved better than this.

Marisa looked positively stunning in a pale-pink sundress that was cinched at her slender waist and emphasized the lush fullness of her breasts and hips.

She stood just inside the door with the boys on either side of her while Jack made the necessary arrangements for the ceremony.

There were a dozen wedding packages to pick from when it came to the actual ceremony. Aware that this was nothing but a business deal, he picked one that would let her carry a nosegay of roses but had fewer of the romantic accoutrements.

The minister had the scent of booze clinging to him, and the witness would be a paid stranger. It all felt slightly seedy.

Jack would have walked out but it was already after five and the boys had forgone their nap and were now getting cranky.

He also didn't want to give himself too much time to think, too much opportunity to let reason take over. He had no idea if this was a mistake or not, but he told himself that if it gave him an edge in a custody battle, then it couldn't be a mistake.

Still, he realized that Marisa should be wearing a white gown of ribbons and lace, and she should be exchanging vows with a man she loved beyond reason.

He wore a suit and tie for the occasion, but he had a feeling he also wore the expression of a deer caught in the headlights.

With the arrangements made and the ceremony paid for, he walked back to where she stood. "Last chance to bail," he said.

She smiled, but the gesture looked slightly forced. "I'm not going anywhere until this is done." She picked up David in her arms, and the toddler wrapped his arms around her neck and laid his head on her shoulder. "Let's just get it finished. The boys are getting hungry and tired."

It took fifteen minutes for Marisa to become Mrs. Jack Cortland. She held David during the brief ceremony, and Jack held Mick.

She only seemed to get emotional once and that was when Jack slipped his mother's wedding ring onto her finger. He'd never given it to Candace, who he'd known would have laughed at the small size of the diamond.

At the end of the ceremony the minister clapped Jack on the back as he walked them out of the chapel and told him he'd always been a big fan of Creation.

Thankfully there were no paparazzi hanging around outside so he didn't have to worry about their wedding becoming a tabloid story.

"I told Betty before we left that we'd be dining out tonight," Jack said as the four of them stepped outside the small chapel. "I thought we could grab a bite at one of the casino buffets or restaurants." He would have never attempted a meal out with the kids before Marisa had arrived and worked her magic with them.

"That's fine, although a restaurant would probably be easier than a buffet with the boys," she replied. David was no longer in her arms but at her side. She held his hand in hers, and in her other hand she clutched the bouquet of pink roses that had come with the wedding ceremony.

It was over a quiet dinner that Jack explained to the boys that Marisa was going to be their new mommy. David seemed to take it all in stride, but Mick looked at her worriedly.

"If you're our new mommy, does that mean you're going to go away?" he asked. His big blue eyes held far too much worry for a little boy.

"No, honey. I don't plan on going away," she replied. "Hopefully we're all going to be together for a very long time."

That seemed to satisfy Mick, who turned his concentration on dipping his French fries into the ocean of ketchup that pooled on his plate.

Marisa was unusually quiet during the meal. Jack watched her easy, loving interaction with David and Mick, and that eased the faint uncertainty that somehow they had made a mistake.

He wasn't worried about the mistake affecting him in a negative way. He'd made enough mistakes in his life to fill a book and had managed to survive them all.

But, he worried about Marisa. She might believe she was in this scheme wholeheartedly now, but how long could a woman exist happily in a loveless situation with just the comfort of two little boys?

There would come a day when she might regret not having a man in her life that she loved, when the love of two little boys just wasn't enough.

He tried to tamp down the simmer of desire that he always felt when he was around her. He had to put the memory of the kisses they had shared out of his mind.

She'd made it clear that this was strictly a platonic union and that the sleeping arrangements would remain the same.

She'd also emphasized that she was agreeing to this because of her own needs and the needs of his sons. She hadn't mentioned his needs at all when she'd made the offer.

Dinner was pleasant, and when they were finished eating they walked back to where they had parked his car. David was once again in Marisa's arms, and Mick rode on Jack's back.

Within the first five minutes of being buckled into their car seats, the boys were both sound asleep. As Jack headed back to the ranch, he cast a quick glance at Marisa, wondering what she was thinking, if perhaps she was already regretting the decision she had made.

"You okay?" he asked.

She turned and smiled at him. She looked relaxed, not stressed. "I'm fine. What about you?"

"I'm good. I think I'm just having a hard time processing what we just did."

He felt her gaze lingering on him. "This is going to be far more difficult on you than it is on me, Jack."

"And why is that?"

"Sex." The word hung in the air.

He shot her a quick glance, fast enough to catch the charming blush that colored her cheeks. "What about it?"

"I know how important it is to most men, but it can't be an issue between us. Getting involved in a physical relationship will only complicate things if this all falls apart." She frowned thoughtfully. "If this condition really bothers you, I suppose it would be okay for you to have an affair if you could do it as discreetly as possible."

He was stunned by her words and by the fact that she would think so little of herself as to agree to such a thing. "I was married to Candace for a long time and never cheated on her. During all my years of partying, I might have done a lot of morally questionable things but I never knowingly slept with a married woman.

"I won't have an affair, Marisa, and I'll respect your wishes about not having a physical relationship with you." He offered her a smile. "Contrary to popular myth, going without sex does not kill a man."

Turning onto the road that would lead them home, he offered her another smile. "However, if you ever change your mind about the no-sex part of this relationship, I hope I'll be the first to know."

"Trust me, you'll be the very first person I tell." Once again deep color filled her cheeks, and he wanted nothing more than to take her in his arms and show her what she'd be missing.

He was definitely going to have to take up splitting wood or something equally physical to ease the burn of the desire she stirred inside him.

He could do it. He would do whatever it took to

keep Marisa in his life. He would do whatever it took to make sure that his boys stayed in his custody, and if that meant living in a sexless marriage, he would do that.

Once they were home Marisa went into her bedroom to change her clothes, and Jack took the boys into the bathroom for a bath and to get them into their pajamas.

The tub was filled with bubbles, and the two boys splashed like fish. They wore the bubbles on their head and on their chins like little white beards.

"Look, Jack." Mick giggled as he built a tower of bubbles on his head. "It's a hat."

"Watch me, Jack," David exclaimed, vying for attention with his brother. He put his face into the water and blew, then raised his head and grinned with obvious pride.

"That's great, David, and Mick, I love your hat," he replied.

Love buoyed up inside him. He couldn't lose them. He needed them in his life and he liked to believe that they needed him.

By the time he got them out of the tub and dried and dressed, he was as wet as they had been. He handed them off to Marisa at the doorway so she could tuck them in and he could change his drenched shirt.

In his bedroom he pulled on a clean white T-shirt, then stood in the boys' bedroom door as Marisa got them into their beds.

"If you're our new mommy, then can we call you Mommy?" Mick asked her as she leaned over to give him a kiss on the forehead.

Marisa stood in obvious surprise and glanced at Jack. He shrugged to indicate that it was her call. She bent down next to Mick and smoothed a strand of his hair away from his face. "I think you should call me whatever you feel comfortable with," she said.

"And you'll be here in the morning when I wake up?" he asked.

Jack's heart squeezed. They had never asked about Candace in the months that he'd had them, and Mick's question indicated to Jack that there had been many mornings when the boys had awakened and not had their mother there.

"I'll be here," Marisa answered simply.

"You promise?" he asked.

"I promise," she replied.

"Okay, then good night, Mommy," he said with a sleepy sigh.

"Now me!" David exclaimed. "Kiss me good-night."

Marisa laughed and quickly kissed Mick on the forehead then moved to David's bedside. "'Night, Mommy," he said and Jack's heart squeezed even tighter.

"Now my turn," he said as Marisa moved toward the door. "Good night, son," he said to Mick as he bent down to kiss him.

"Good night, Daddy," Mick replied.

For a moment Jack remained frozen as a joy he'd never known coursed through him. Daddy. Finally, he'd heard that word from his son's mouth. Never had a single word sounded so sweet.

When David said the same thing, he left the room with a sense of wonderment. As he and Marisa walked out in the hallway he caught her by the shoulders and stared at her for a long moment.

"You did this," he whispered. "I don't know how you did it, but you accomplished a miracle."

She smiled, her eyes shining brightly. "It's no miracle, Jack. They love you, and finally they're willing to trust you. I didn't do this, you did."

He couldn't control himself. His joy was so great he had to kiss her. He grabbed her into his arms and commandeered her lips with his.

For a moment he could think of nothing but the happiness in his soul and the pleasure of her warm lips beneath his.

It was only when he felt her stiffen against him that he dropped his hands and stepped back from her. Jeez, they hadn't even been married five hours and already he had stepped over the line.

"I'm sorry," he said awkwardly. "I just got carried away with the moment. I won't let it happen again." He didn't wait for her reply but instead walked down the hallway to his bedroom.

Chapter 9

Marisa stood on the porch and watched the car pulling away from the house. She sighed in exhaustion. She'd arranged for a playdate for the boys and had spent the morning entertaining not two but four rambunctious, energetic little boys.

She was about to turn and go back into the house when she saw Sam and Max Burrow standing near the barn, their gazes directed at her. A small chill worked its way up her back.

During the course of the past week since the marriage, she'd felt them staring at her far too often. It gave her a creepy, unsettled feeling, and she couldn't help but wonder if Jack had vented his rage about who was feeding Harold information on the wrong person.

She closed the front door and set the alarm, then collapsed on the sofa in the living room, where Mick and David were playing with their truck collection.

The visitors had been previous charges of Marisa, the two sons of Margaret and John Covewell, who worked at one of the casinos. She'd worked for them for four months, until they had gotten themselves into a financial position where Margaret could be a stay-at-home mom.

Although the first hour had been a little rough as David and Mick weren't used to sharing either toys or attention with any other children, the last hour had gone remarkably smoothly.

Jack was outside somewhere. In the past week they had fallen into a routine that allowed him to work on the ranch during the day, then spend his late afternoon and evenings with the boys.

There had been no more interaction between Jack and Kent, and Marisa knew the rift weighed heavy on Jack's mind. They still had no idea what the man had wanted who had tried to break into the house, but thankfully nothing alarming had happened since then.

That wasn't exactly true, she thought. The most alarming thing happening in her life at the moment was the growing intensity of her desire for Jack.

It was hotter than anything she'd ever felt for her

boyfriend in college. They were all living like a happy family, but at night when she climbed into her lonely bed she ached for something more. And when she finally fell asleep it was to erotic dreams of making love with Jack.

In those dreams it wasn't just the sex that overwhelmed her. It was the fact that Jack whispered his love for her—a love that had nothing to do with his sons but rather that indefinable emotion between a man and a woman.

What she had to remember was that she was just a means to an end to better his chances if a custody battle should ensue. Their relationship was only about the boys, not about love.

Seeing that the boys were playing well together, she went into the kitchen, where Betty was finishing up the preparation of the evening meal.

"Is there anything I can do to help?" she asked.

Betty looked at her as if she'd just suggested murder. The old woman had been particularly cantankerous over the past week. "Do I look like I need help?" she asked. "Have you noticed the food not tasting right lately? Am I getting the meals ready on time?"

"No, I mean yes." Marisa frowned. "Betty, I didn't ask because I think you needed my help. I just wondered if you'd like any help."

Betty set down the knife she'd been using to cut up vegetables. "Just tell me now. Am I going to lose my job?"

Marisa looked at her in surprise. "Why would you ask?"

Betty shrugged her skinny shoulders. "With you and Jack married now, I've been wondering when you'd decide to take over everything in the house."

"I have no intention of taking over your job," Marisa assured her. "To be perfectly honest with you, there are some things I do very well, but I never really got the hang of cooking."

The taut line of Betty's mouth relaxed, and she picked up the paring knife once again. "It's not that hard if you put your mind to it."

Marisa leaned a hip against the counter. "How well do you know Sam and Max?" she asked suddenly.

"I've known those two since they were teenagers. Why?"

"I was just curious about what kind of men they were." Marisa didn't want to say that she had questions about their loyalty to Jack, and she definitely didn't want to mention that the two occasionally gave her the creeps.

"They're good men, not too bright but hard workers. Jack could do a lot worse."

At that moment there was a cry from the living room, and Marisa rushed from the kitchen to tend to a fight between the two brothers.

That night after the boys had been tucked into bed, Marisa and Jack sat in the living room as was their custom.

"Are you okay?" she asked. He'd been unusually quiet the entire evening.

"I'm fine. Why?"

"You just seem like you have a lot on your mind." She wondered if he was regretting the marriage. He'd reached a place with the boys where they would have been fine without her. Jack had learned to be consistent with discipline, and the boys had begun to trust him to be there for them.

He leaned back in his chair and released an audible sigh. "Things have been quiet for the past week. I haven't received even one phone call from Harold. I somehow feel like it's the calm before the storm."

"Have you heard from Kent?" she asked.

He shook his head, his eyes deepening in hue. There was no question that the topic of Kent hurt him. "But I didn't expect to."

"Maybe you should talk to him again, Jack. It would be a shame to throw away all those years of friendship that the two of you shared, especially given the fact that we don't even know for sure if he is the one who is feeding Harold information."

He rubbed two fingers across his forehead, as if fighting a headache. "I've lost all objectivity about all of this. Maybe you're right. Maybe I need to sit down with Kent and talk. I'll go over to his place tomorrow." He dropped his hand from his forehead and smiled at her.

That smile of his warmed a place inside her that no other smile had done. "You know, just because we got married doesn't mean you can't still pursue your dream of owning your own nanny agency," he said.

"To be honest, I haven't even thought about it for the past couple of weeks," she admitted. "But it is something I'd like to do. I'd need to create a Web site and do some advertising, and I'd also need to interview prospective employees but it's all something I could do from the house. I'd never have to leave the boys."

"I want you to do what makes you happy, Marisa." His deep voice was as soft as a caress. "You've already sacrificed so much for me. I'll support whatever it is you want to do as far as an agency is concerned."

It was far more difficult than she'd expected to maintain an emotional distance from him. She'd tried desperately since the moment she'd met him to keep herself detached, to ignore the simmering burn he evoked in her. But it was getting more arduous with each day that passed.

"I think I'll go to bed," she said, releasing a tired sigh. "The playdate today exhausted me." At that moment Mick cried out, obviously suffering from one of his nightmares.

"I'll take care of him," Jack said and got up from his chair. As Marisa went into her bedroom Jack disappeared into the boys' room.

She went into her bathroom and got undressed and into her silky nightgown, then pulled her robe around her and crept out into the hallway just outside the boys' bedroom.

Her breath caught in her chest as she heard Jack singing, his deep, melodious voice whispering of circus clowns and treasures found, of big balloons and smiling moons.

Marisa leaned with her back against the hallway wall and closed her eyes as warmth rushed through her. It was a warmth coupled with a horrible sense of dread as she realized she'd fallen hopelessly in love with her husband.

Jack sang until Mick fell back asleep. He remained in the chair next to the bed for a long moment, breathing in the scent of his boys, then quietly got up and left the room.

He nearly collided with Marisa, who was standing in the hallway just outside. She looked up at him with her liquid brown eyes, and the smile that curved her lips made his heart pound just a bit.

"That was beautiful," she said, her voice a husky whisper.

"I might not be good at a lot of things, but I always could sing," he replied. Every muscle in his body tensed as she didn't move away. He feared he might lose his mind if she didn't stop looking at him like that.

He shifted from one foot to the other. "Well, I guess I'll just say good-night," he finally said. He started to walk by her to return to the living room, but she stopped him by placing her delicate hand on his forearm.

"Jack?" Her eyes were luminous as she gazed up at him.

"Yeah?" The air between them seemed to shimmer with an energy that made it difficult for him to breathe.

She moistened her lips with the tip of her tongue, and Jack felt his blood pressure shoot through the ceiling. "I told you that you'd be the first to know if I changed my mind," she said.

Jack shoved his hands in his jean pockets, afraid of where they might roam, afraid that he might misunderstand what she was talking about. "Changed your mind about what?" He fought the urge to cough to clear away the huskiness of his throat.

A wild desire had crashed through him the moment she'd touched her lips with her tongue. The thin cotton robe she wore did nothing to hide her curves, and the tiny peek of red silk he saw only further heated the blood rushing through his veins.

"About not having anything physical between us." Her cheeks flamed, but she held his gaze with an uplifted chin. "I mean, if you were interested in having something physical between us, I wouldn't be upset."

Carla Cassidy 137

"If I'm interested?" He pulled his hands from his pockets. "Marisa, I've been interested in a physical relationship with you since the moment you walked through my front door."

He felt frozen in place, afraid to move too fast, afraid to move too slow, scared somehow that he'd do something to shatter the moment and that gorgeous light in her eyes.

She took a step closer to him, engulfing him in that delicious scent of hers. "So do you intend to do something about it or are you just going to stand there and stare at me?"

Her upper lip trembled slightly, letting him know that she was nervous, that she was putting herself on the line and wasn't sure what reaction she might get from him.

He pulled her into his arms and placed his lips against hers. Softly, tenderly he kissed her as he cradled her against him. But the kiss didn't remain soft or tender. As she wrapped her arms around his neck and opened her mouth against his, his need roared through him like a loosened beast.

He wanted to devour her. He felt as if he'd been on a slow burn since the moment they'd met, and her sudden acquiescence was the fuel that exploded that simmer into a raging inferno.

He broke the kiss, wanting to get her into his bedroom, into his bed before she changed her mind.

As he stepped back from her he reached for her

hand and led her down the hallway toward his bedroom. She followed him without hesitation, but her hand trembled slightly in his.

The bedside lamp was on in his room, casting a faint golden light on the king-size bed he hadn't made that morning.

He dropped her hand and looked at her. As much as he needed to take what he wanted from her, he gave her one last chance to halt what they were about to do.

"Marisa, this wasn't what you offered to me when you agreed to marry me. I don't want to take advantage of you," he rasped out. "I want you, but I don't want you to feel pressured in any way to do this."

She didn't reply. She untied the belt at her waist and allowed the robe to fall to the floor behind her. The red silk nightgown hit her mid-thigh, and the deep V-neck exposed the swell of her upper breasts.

Jack bit back the moan that tried to escape him as he saw that her nipples were already hard and pressed tauntingly against the silk material.

"Trust me, Jack. I never do anything I don't want to do." She took a step closer to him, her eyes a pool of darkness that he could easily submerge himself in.

He felt as if he were in a fog as he grabbed her to him once again, his hands sliding down the silky gown to grab her buttocks and pull her as close to him as possible.

Once again their lips met in a hot, wild kiss that

had him hungering for more. He slid his mouth from hers and instead rained kisses across her jaw and down the length of her neck. She gasped in pleasure as he found a sensitive place just behind her ear.

The sound of her gasp ignited the flames inside him even more, and he stumbled back from her and yanked his T-shirt over his head.

At one time he might have been smooth, but it had been so long and he felt like a teenager preparing for his very first time. His fingers fumbled with his button fly as she pulled the nightgown over her head and slid in under the sheets.

He kicked off his shoes and finally got out of his pants, and then he tore off his socks and joined her in the bed. She was clad only in a little pair of red panties and he in a pair of briefs, but as they came together their naked skin warmed with the intimate contact.

He tangled his hands in her luxurious hair as he kissed her hungrily. She returned his kiss with a fever of her own, her tongue swirling with his as she pressed her naked breasts against his chest.

It didn't take long for Jack to want more than kissing. He rolled her over on her back and captured the tip of one of her breasts in his mouth. Gasping with pleasure, she writhed beneath him.

He laved first one nipple, then the other, fired up by the sounds she made as he cupped her breasts and made love to them.

She didn't remain a passive partner. Her hands roamed his body. She clutched his shoulders, then smoothed her palms down the length of his back.

Jack had forgotten the wonder of human touch, of body heat shared. But that wonder all came rushing back as their foreplay grew more intimate.

Smoothing his hand down the flat of her stomach, his heart pumped fast and furious. As he reached the waist of her panties, he felt her catch her breath.

He glanced at her, and her eyes glowed almost feral in the splash of illumination from the lamp. He held her gaze as he pressed his hand against her panties, her heat radiating out from the wispy material.

Even though he knew she was turned on, he sensed that she was holding back. He wanted her mindless. He wanted that control to shatter, wanted her to go to the place where there was nothing in the world but him and what they were sharing.

He caressed her through the panties, and a low moan escaped her lips as she thrust her hips upward to meet his touch.

Jack was quickly reaching the end of his own control. He grabbed hold of the sides of her panties and pulled them down. She aided him by rising up, her eyes filled with urgency.

He pulled off his own briefs and tossed them to the floor, then gathered her back in his arms for another soul-searing kiss.

As he kissed her, she reached down and closed her fingers around his arousal. The intimate touch nearly undid him. He grabbed her wrist. "Don't," he said in a raw whisper. "If you touch me for another second it will all be over."

Her eyes flared slightly, and she pulled her hand away from him as he once again began to caress her intimately. He moved his fingers against her moist heat, wanting her to tumble off the edge of reason, fall into the place where thought wasn't possible.

"Let go," he said softly. "Marisa, just let go."

She gasped and closed her eyes, and he felt her relaxing, welcoming his touch without reservation.

It didn't take long before her body began to tense and her breathing grew ragged. She arched her hips, and he felt the wave of release that shuddered through her.

Before she had a chance to recover he moved between her thighs. Her eyes opened and she looked up at him, but by the wild glaze there he knew she wasn't seeing him. She was lost in the sensual pleasure, and as he entered her, he let go of the last of his own control.

Chapter 10

Marisa awoke first. The faint glow of dawn crept into the window as she lay spooned against Jack. One of his arms was flung across her waist, and for just one sleepy moment she felt at peace and she felt loved.

Illusion, she told herself. Still, she didn't move, unwilling to break this magical spell until it was absolutely necessary.

Making love with Jack had been beyond anything she'd imagined. She'd expected passion. She'd anticipated fast and hot and wild. What she hadn't expected was his tenderness.

And there had been a wealth of tenderness. She

closed her eyes, her head still filled with thoughts of Jack.

She recognized that the hard-rocking, headbanging drummer that he'd once been had been a facade. The real Jack Cortland was a sensitive man who cared deeply about family and friends and perhaps maybe a little bit about her.

But she had no illusions about what had occurred between them the night before. It had been sex. Nothing more, nothing less. It had been an explosion of the sexual tension that had existed between them from the moment they'd met.

Jack wasn't in love with her. He might love her for what she was doing for him—and for the boys. But there was a difference between loving somebody and being in love with somebody.

She was in love with Jack, in a way she'd never been with Tom in college, but she had a terrible feeling that ultimately this all would eventually end in her heartbreak.

One day at a time, she told herself. Her days would be filled with taking care of Mick and David and building the business she'd dreamed of owning. And her nights—she wasn't sure where she'd be spending them, although she knew where she wanted to be…right here beside Jack.

His hands smoothed down the outside of her thigh, letting her know he was awake. "Good morning," he whispered against the back of her neck, his warm breath sending a shiver of pleasure through her.

She told herself she should get up and get out of his arms, but she remained where she was as she murmured a good-morning back to him.

She'd never had a morning with Tom. She'd never awakened in his arms after a night of lovemaking. She'd been nothing more to him than a quick convenience, and she had a feeling that's what she had become with Jack.

This thought drove her out of his arms and out of the bed. She grabbed her robe from the floor and pulled it around her nakedness.

"Gee, I was kind of looking forward to an encore," he said as he sat up.

He looked roguishly appealing with his hair tousled from sleep and a lazy, sexy smile curving his lips. His smile fell as he studied her features in the semidarkness of the room. "Please don't tell me you have morning-after regrets."

"No, no regrets," she replied. It was true; there was no way she could regret making love with him. "I just have a lot of things I want to get done today, and I thought I'd get a head start before the boys got up."

"You going to work on your business venture?" he asked curiously. She nodded and belted her robe more firmly around her waist. His smile fell. "We haven't talked about what you intend to do with your house. Are you planning on selling it?"

She thought of the little bungalow her parents had bought her as a college graduation present. She loved the little house, but if this had been a real marriage she would have sold it in a minute and completely melded her life with that of her husband's.

But this *wasn't* a real marriage, and she wasn't comfortable giving up everything without a crystal ball to see into the future.

"I don't plan on doing anything with it for a while," she replied. "I'm going to go shower. I'll see you in the kitchen in a few minutes." She left the room and went down the hallway to her own bedroom.

Eventually if she remained here with Jack and the boys she'd want some of the things from her house. But even though she'd made a commitment to remain here, in the back of her mind she couldn't help but feel that this whole arrangement was temporary. Keeping her house was a safety net in case everything fell apart.

The morning passed as always with Jack out on the ranch with his men and Marisa entertaining the boys and taking care of some of the housework. It was Saturday so they were on their own for meals. Breakfast was cereal, lunch was sandwiches and Marisa had ambitious plans to make spaghetti sauce for dinner.

It was when the boys went down for a nap that Jack told her he was going over to Kent's to have a talk.

"Good, I'm glad," she replied as she sank down onto the sofa.

He frowned thoughtfully. "I keep thinking about how it was when I moved back here after the divorce. I was in bad shape, and if it wasn't for Kent I'm not sure I would have survived." He leaned against the chair, and his gray eyes gazed at her thoughtfully. "What about your friends, Marisa? I don't ever hear you talking on the phone with anyone except your aunt and occasionally your parents."

"After I lost the baby, I pretty much withdrew from everyone." Emotion swelled in her chest as she remembered those dark days after the miscarriage. "I went through a period of mourning followed by a depression."

She pulled her legs up beneath her and leaned her head back against the cushion. "My friends didn't seem to understand that this wasn't something I could just put behind me, and they weren't comfortable with my grief. By the time I graduated from college I'd pretty well isolated myself, then I immediately began to work as a nanny. That kept me too busy to miss any of my friends."

She smiled at him, wanting to take away the frown that tugged his eyebrows low. "Don't look so worried, Jack. I'm relatively well-adjusted, and I'm open to the possibility of making new friends. Go on, get out of here and make peace with your friend."

"I shouldn't be too long," he said as he headed for the front door.

"Take whatever time you need. I'm going to do a little work on the computer, then see about making a pot of the best spaghetti you've ever eaten."

He grinned at her. "Sounds great. I'll see you later. Don't forget to set the alarm after I leave."

The minute he went out the door she pulled herself off the sofa and reset the alarm, then returned to her bedroom, where her laptop was plugged in.

She'd just started working on a Web site for her nanny agency when Jack had first hired her, and she eagerly dove back into it now. She tinkered with it for a half hour before the boys awakened from their naps.

As they played in the living room she made a call to the newspaper to place an ad for young women interested in becoming nannies, then joined the boys in the middle of the floor for playtime.

They were in the process of building a fort from several empty cardboard boxes when there was a knock on the door.

She looked out to see Patrick standing on the porch. What was he doing here? As she reached for the doorknob the ring that Jack had placed on her finger sparkled in the sunlight.

"Patrick." She greeted him with a cautious smile. "What a surprise."

"Hi, Marisa. I just thought I'd stop by and see

how you were getting along." He hesitated a moment, then offered her a smile. "Can I come in?"

She opened the door wider to allow him inside. "Come on into the living room. We were just in the process of building a fort."

Mick and David barely paid attention to Patrick as they colored the boxes in shades of brown and black.

"I miss you, Marisa," Patrick said. "I've given you a little time, and I was hoping that maybe you changed your mind about me…about us."

Marisa drew a deep breath. She had to tell him about marrying Jack, but she had to make a fast decision about what, exactly, she intended to tell him.

For some reason her pride wouldn't allow her to tell him the truth, that she and Jack had made a business arrangement for the sake of the two little boys who were now coloring their fort with purple and red crayons.

"Patrick, I'm sorry. I haven't changed my mind. In fact, as crazy as it sounds, I've fallen in love with Jack, and he's fallen in love with me. Last week we got married."

For a moment he looked stunned. "Wow, that was really fast. Are you sure you haven't made a mistake?"

"Positive," she replied without hesitation. "I've never been happier." The minute the words left her mouth she knew they were true. She had no idea how long this happiness would last, but she intended to embrace it for as long as it existed.

"Then I guess I'm happy for you," he said with a tight smile.

She relaxed. "Thanks."

"Well, then I guess I should get out of here." He headed for the door then paused and turned back to her. "I've heard Jack has a whole bunch of Creation memorabilia in the barn. Do you think I could take a peek at it?"

Marisa remembered him telling her that he'd once been a fan. "I guess it would be all right. I don't think Jack would mind. Boys, you want to go to the barn for a few minutes?" Just as she expected, the two raced to her side.

"Mick and David, you remember Patrick," Marisa said.

The boys murmured hellos, and Patrick raised a dark eyebrow. "Mick and David, as in Jagger and Bowie?"

She smiled. "That's right. Apparently Candace was a big fan of the legendary rock idols. Come on, let's take a walk."

The four of them left the house, the boys jumping and skipping with boyish energy. "I don't know how you keep up with them," Patrick exclaimed. There was a suppressed impatience to his tone that made her think perhaps Patrick wasn't so fond of children.

They would have never had a chance for a future together, she thought. One way or another children would have always been a big part of her life.

Neither Sam nor Max were in sight as they reached the barn. She figured the two were out someplace on the acreage. Jack had told her they were mending a section of fence almost two miles from the house.

The barn door creaked open, and the four of them entered. Patrick gasped in amazement. "My God, I'd heard rumors that he had a bunch of stuff in here, but this is amazing."

Marisa smiled as she watched him move around the room. David headed directly to the drums, and Mick found the dolls that he'd played with the last time they had been inside the building.

As he began to bang on the cymbal, Patrick winced. "Can you make him stop that?" he said, a touch of irritation in his voice.

Marisa looked at Patrick in surprise. She was definitely seeing a side of him she didn't find attractive. "David, come here, honey," she said, but he ignored her.

"Hey, I've got an idea," Patrick said. He pulled a chair in front of him and smiled at Marisa. "Why don't we play a game of cops and robbers?" He reached into his pocket and pulled out a small revolver. "Sit down, Marisa," he said, all attempt at levity gone.

She stared at him in incomprehension. "What are you doing? Patrick, what's going on?" Her heart thumped painfully hard in her chest.

"I said sit down," he replied. "You don't want me to get angry and upset the kids."

She sank down on the chair, almost hypnotized by the weapon in his hand. "Is this about me breaking up with you?" she asked.

"Don't be stupid," he exclaimed as he pulled a length of rope from his pocket. "Hey, boys, let's play a game and tie up Marisa." He leaned closer to her ear. "If you don't cooperate I'll kill them both."

The low menace in his voice coupled with the hard glaze of his eyes made her believe him and her blood ran cold. "Patrick, please. Jack is going to be home at any moment. I don't understand. Why are you doing this?"

As he began to bind her hands behind her, the boys came to stand nearby, watching as Patrick tied her to the chair.

"Jack won't be home anytime soon," he said. "My partner will make sure he doesn't arrive here until it's too late."

He didn't speak again until both her hands and feet were bound to the chair. As he stepped back from her she tried to pull her hands free, but there was no give in the rope.

"Patrick, why are you doing this?" She tried to keep her voice as calm as possible, not wanting to frighten Mick and David, who were watching the two of them with widened eyes.

He drew himself up straight and proud. "My name isn't Patrick. Over the years I've had lots of names and lots of identities, but my real name is Paz Marquez. It was my father who found the diamond, The Tears of the Quetzal. It should have belonged to him, but Joseph Rothchild, Harold's father, found out about it."

Paz's handsome face twisted into a mask of hatred so intense it nearly stole Marisa's breath away. "Joseph killed my father. He buried him alive in a cave and walked away with the diamond. I got it back from Candace the night I murdered her, but it slipped through my fingers once again…and I've been targeting the Rothchilds ever since."

Marisa gasped. He'd killed before. He'd killed Candace. And clearly he was responsible for those other mysterious acts against the family that had been splashed all over the tabloids. Her sense of danger rose dramatically as fear lodged in her throat.

"I finally got it back." He smiled, and it was a cruel, hard gesture. "It's back where it belongs in my possession."

"Patrick, I had nothing to do with any of this. The boys had nothing to do with it. Let us go." Her voice trembled with terror.

"The boys have *everything* to do with this," he replied, seething anger still rife in his voice. "Right,

Mick? Right, David?" He cast the boys a friendly smile. "I figure they're worth at least a million a piece. Their grandfather is easily capable of paying that, and it's the least of what he owes me."

The blood that had been cold inside her turned even icier. "Patrick, you have the Rothchild ring. Isn't that enough? You have the diamond you said belonged to your father."

"No, it's not enough." His hands tightened into fists at his sides. "I want the Rothchilds' blood. I want their tears. I want them to know the kind of pain I've known because of them."

She struggled against the ropes as a deep sob wrenched from her. She had to do something. She had to save the boys.

The only thing she could do was scream and hope that either Sam or Max might hear her cry. The shriek that ripped out of her came from her soul. She never saw it coming, but she felt the crashing blow that landed on the side of her head...then nothing.

Pain brought her back to consciousness, an excruciating pain in her skull that made her feel nauseous.

As she opened her eyes she realized two things had changed. There was now duct tape plastered across her mouth, and the boys were nowhere in sight.

Dear God, where was Mick and David? What had he done with them? With a new fervor she pulled against the ropes that held her tight in the chair.

"Ah, I see you're back." Patrick stood in front of her, a large red can held in his hand.

Frantically she struggled to get free, screaming into the tape with a growing sense of horror. She cried out as the chair toppled to its side with her still bound to it. She lay with the side of her face pressed against the ground, and tears began to burn in her eyes.

"It's been nice knowing you, Marisa," Patrick said from someplace behind her. "Those two little boys are my ticket to wealth. Unfortunately you're worth nothing. Still, I'm hoping your death will make both Jack and Harold shed a tear or two."

She realized at that moment that it wasn't money that drove Paz, it was a rage-driven need for revenge. She heard the splash of liquid and instantly smelled the odor of gasoline. Fire! He intended to set her on fire.

The scent of the gasoline grew stronger as he continued to splash the liquid around the perimeter of the barn.

Marisa tried desperately to get herself untied, but it was a futile effort. Her wrists and ankles burned, and the fumes from the fuel were almost overwhelming.

Mick! David! Her heart cried out. She felt little fear for herself as her concentration was on the two little boys she'd grown to love with all her heart.

Jack, where are you? Come save your babies! Come save me!

"I guess this is goodbye, Marisa," Patrick said from behind her. She heard the strike of a match, then the loud whoosh of flames. The barn door slammed shut, leaving her alone with the fire that within seconds burned with a crackling heat.

Smoke billowed around her, making it difficult for her to see, almost impossible for her to breathe. She coughed and choked against the gag, and her lungs felt as if they were about to explode.

Dark shadows closed in, obscuring her vision altogether as unconsciousness reached out to her. Her last conscious thought was the bitter regret that somehow she'd brought a monster to Jack's door.

Chapter 11

It had taken a week for Rita to learn that Patrick Moore, the man Marisa had been dating, didn't exist.

She'd begun to get suspicious about him when she'd realized the last time she'd seen the ring had been just before he and Marisa had come over for dinner.

Rita knew her niece would never enter her office, and certainly would never take something that didn't belong to her. But she couldn't help but recall that Patrick had left the two women while they'd been clearing the dishes, supposedly to go to the bathroom, and gut instinct warned her that Patrick might have stolen the ring. However, she was still trying to wrap her brain around how he could have discovered where the ring was stashed and how he'd managed to seize it from a locked gun safe. This was clearly the work of a professional...

Yesterday she'd called the accounting agency where she knew Patrick worked, only to discover that he had quit his job there two weeks before. She'd gotten an address from them and had gone to the location late last night, only to discover that it was an empty lot on the outskirts of town.

While she stood on that vacant lot, a new fear had gripped her. Who was Patrick Moore, and why would he have a false address? It was something a criminal would do.

Rita had tried to call Marisa a few minutes ago to see if she could give her any information that might lead Rita to the young man's real identity or home address, but there had been no answer at Cortland's house.

Rita needed to recover that ring. Her career depended on it. But, more than that, she needed to alert Marisa that Patrick Moore wasn't the wonderful man they'd thought he was.

She had a sick feeling in her heart, one that usually portended something bad about to happen. She picked up the phone and dialed the Cortland ranch again. This time she just needed to check to make sure that Marisa was all right.

She sighed in frustration when there was still no

answer. She grabbed her keys and headed for her apartment door, unable to just sit still and do nothing.

She'd start with the accounting agency and see what Patrick's associates could tell her about the man that might lead to his whereabouts and the truth of his real identity.

"I really need to get back home," Jack said for the third time in the past fifteen minutes. He'd already been at Kent's for over an hour and a half. What had begun as a healing of the rift between the two men had transformed into a walk down memory lane.

"Hey, remember that time we played that gig in Riverside and the owner of the place paid us in beer?" Kent asked, obviously not ready to call a halt to the conversation.

Jack stood from the chair where he'd been sitting in Kent's tiny living room. "Yeah, I remember. We were all underage, and we ended up drunk for the next two days. Kent, I really gotta go. I need to get home to the kids."

Kent glanced at his watch and then stood as well. "Okay, I guess if you have to take off…"

"I really do," Jack replied.

"Hey, man, thanks for coming by," Kent said as the two of them stepped out on the front porch. "I really felt bad about our argument. I wish I knew who was feeding Harold information, but you should know I'd never do anything to hurt you." He held out a hand, and Jack gripped it in a firm hand-shake.

Minutes later as Jack headed back home, he still wasn't sure that he trusted Kent. Certainly Kent had mouthed all the right words, proclaiming his inno-cence with a resounding fervor, but Jack wasn't sure if it was just an act.

He realized that until he knew the truth of who Harold was talking to, the only thing he and Marisa could do was make certain nothing bad happened. If a mole had nothing to talk about, then he'd have to remain silent.

His thoughts turned to Marisa and what they had shared the night before. It had been amazing. They had fit together as naturally as if they'd been made for one another. Even now, just thinking about it, he felt himself getting aroused.

She had transformed his life and he would forever be grateful to her for all that she had done.

But the feeling that filled his heart when he thought about her had little to do with gratitude. He cared about her. He loved to see the light of a smile dance on her lips and shine from her eyes. The sound of her laughter filled him with a warmth he hadn't felt for a very long time.

Still, he wasn't convinced she was in his life for the long-term. If he needed any evidence of that it was the fact that she wasn't willing to give up her house. She was hedging her bets, making certain she had a fast and easy escape route if things went bad.

Funny how the thought of her not being in his home, in his life, filled him with regret.

He loved what she had done with his boys, but more than that he loved what she had done for him. She'd made him believe he could be the kind of man he wanted to be. She'd given him the confidence to not only embrace parenthood but also to hold close to who he was at his very core.

He saw the smoke as he turned onto the long gravel road that led to his ranch. It billowed upward, a dark gray snake slithering up in the sky.

His heart seemed to stop in his chest as he realized it was his barn that was on fire. He tromped on the accelerator and squealed to a halt in front of the burning building.

Sam and Max were already there with garden hoses spewing ineffectual sprays of water.

"Call the fire department," Jack yelled as he leaped out of his car.

"Already did," Sam replied above the roar of the flames.

Jack didn't give a damn about anything that was in the barn. It was just stuff from his past, things that no longer really mattered to him. But as he thought about how much Mick loved those stupid dolls and David adored the cymbals, he decided to try to get inside and at least retrieve those items.

He grabbed the garden hose from Sam's hand and sprayed himself down. Once he was soaking wet, he burst through the barn doors.

Visibility was next to nothing, and smoke seared his lungs as he raced toward the box where the dolls were kept. It was then that he saw her. Marisa—tied to an overturned chair and still as death.

He cried out in horror and raced to her. A million thoughts raced through his head. What was she doing out here? Who had tied her to the chair?

Overhead the fire raged, and the ominous sound of cracking wood made him realize the roof was about to collapse at any minute.

Instead of taking the time to try to untie her, he made the split-second decision to grab the chair with both hands and dragged it and her toward the door.

Don't be dead. Please don't be dead. The mantra went around and around in his brain as he struggled to get her out of the barn.

He nearly sobbed in relief as he pulled her out into the fresh air and her eyes opened. She began to cough, choking against the duct tape that rode across her lips.

He yanked off the tape, then straightened and looked back at the barn. *The boys. Oh, God, were the boys inside?* Once again his heart felt as if it stopped beating altogether.

"Marisa, are the boys in the barn?" he asked, his heart pounding so loudly he was afraid he might not hear her reply.

A breath whooshed out of him as she shook her head violently. But the relief was short-lived as she clutched him by the arm. "They're gone, Jack. He took them." Once again she was overcome by a spasm of coughing.

In the distance came the sound of sirens drawing closer. Jack leaned down to Marisa, the knot in his chest so tight he could scarcely draw a breath. "Who? Who has the boys, Marisa?"

Tears washed down her smoke-blackened face. "Patrick. Oh, God, Jack. I'm sorry. I'm so sorry." She began to sob as the fire engines pulled up in front of the barn and Jack's cell phone vibrated from his shirt pocket.

He straightened and walked back to his car as he pulled the phone out. The caller ID displayed the caller as anonymous.

"Cortland," he said as he got into his car and shut the door, grateful that the fire trucks had cut their sirens.

"I have your boys. If you go to the police I will kill them. If you talk to anyone in law enforcement, I will kill them. Do you understand?" Patrick's voice was deep and chilling.

Jack wanted to reach through the phone and kill him. He tamped down the rage, knowing that his sons' lives hung in the balance. "I understand. What do you want?"

"Two million dollars."

Jack barked a humorless laugh. "I don't have that kind of money. Don't you remember, I'm an old has-been who blew his cash on drugs and alcohol."

"You might not have it, but you can get it," Patrick replied.

"And how am I supposed to do that?"

"Harold Rothchild will be happy to pay that for the return of his grandchildren. I'll give you until nine o'clock this evening to get it together. I'll be in touch."

The line went dead.

Jack dropped the phone back into his pocket and gripped the steering wheel with both hands. Outside his car, chaos reigned. The firemen were losing the battle with the blazing barn, and Marisa was seated with an oxygen mask over her mouth and nose.

But the scene happening before his eyes had nothing on the drama that unfolded in his head. Mick and David were in danger, and tears stung his eyes as he thought of his precious sons.

His first impulse was to call the police, but as he replayed Patrick's menacing voice in his head he feared the consequences of that particular action. There had been an edge in Patrick's tone that had let Jack know he was capable of harming the boys.

Jack got out of the car and hurried over to Marisa, who pulled the mask off her face and burst into tears as he approached.

He pulled her up off the ground and into his arms,

knowing the particular kind of torture she must be going through.

"I'm sorry. I'm so sorry," she sobbed against his chest. "I couldn't stop him. He said he wanted to see some of your things from your band days. I never thought… I never imagined. He pulled a gun, and there was nothing I could do."

"Shh, it's all right," Jack said as he rubbed her back. "You need to pull yourself together, Marisa, and tell me everything that happened. You need to tell me everything he said."

Maybe he'd said something to her that would provide a clue as to where he had the boys.

She raised her head and looked at him, her brown eyes filled with torment. "He killed Candace, Jack. He told me that he killed her."

Ice rolled through Jack's veins. "Go get in my car," he said to her. "I'll be right there." As she headed for the vehicle he walked over to the fire chief. The fire was still burning, but it was obvious the barn was a complete loss.

Jack told the man in charge that he had to leave but would be in touch in the next day or two. Then he hurried back to his car where Marisa awaited him.

As he started the car Marisa began to tell him everything that had happened from the moment Patrick had appeared on the doorstep.

Jack's blood was cold as ice by the time she

finished telling him everything that lunatic had said. "Where does Patrick live?" he asked her.

"I don't know. He always came to my place." She wrapped her arms around her stomach, as if she were physically ill. "Are you going to call the police?"

"Patrick called me a few minutes ago. He told me he has the boys and if I contact the police he'll kill them." He gripped the steering wheel so tightly he feared he might snap it in half. "I believe him. I'm going to have to take my chances without any police reinforcement."

"He said he had a partner, Jack, and that partner would make sure you didn't get home too quickly. It has to be Kent," she said.

The flames that lit inside Jack's stomach were hotter than the ones that had consumed his barn as he thought of how Kent had stalled him again and again from leaving his place.

If he was going to find his boys, then it was possible the answer was with Kent. He tore down the highway toward Kent's place, the rage inside him building to mammoth proportions.

If anything happened to his boys and Kent had anything to do with it, then Jack would kill him. It was as simple as that.

He pulled up in front of Kent's small farmhouse, and as he got out of the car he was aware of Marisa shadowing just behind him.

The burn in his gut flamed hotter and when Kent opened the door, Jack swung his fist and punched him in the nose. Kent fell backward as blood blossomed and trickled from his nostrils.

"What the hell?" He scrambled to his feet and backed away as Jack came at him again.

"Where are my sons?" Jack roared. He would have hit the man again if Marisa hadn't grabbed on to his arm and held tight.

"I don't know what you're talking about," Kent yelled as he fumbled in his back pocket for a handkerchief. He pressed it against his nose and tried to look belligerent but Jack smelled fear.

"Patrick told me you were his partner just before he tried to burn me alive," Marisa said as her fingers bit into Jack's arm. "He killed Candace, Kent. Your partner is a murderer."

Kent's eyes widened and a gasp exploded out of him. "Nobody was supposed to get hurt," he said. "He promised me that nobody would get hurt."

"What have you done, Kent?" The words came from Jack in a tortured whisper.

"It was supposed to be easy. Just grab the kids, get the ransom then finally live on easy street for the rest of my life," Kent said.

"Why would you do something like this to me?" Jack asked as he stared at the man who was supposed to be his best friend.

Kent took a step backward from him, and his

eyes darkened with a hint of anger. "Because you left me behind. The whole time we were kids we talked about going to L.A. and building a band. Then you took off by yourself and never thought about me again. You had it all, and you left me here with nothing." His voice rose on the last few words. "Damn you, Jack. You just left me behind."

Jack stared at him in stunned surprise. This was about jealousy? "I don't have time for this. Where did he take my boys?"

"I don't know. He was supposed to call me when he had them, but I haven't heard from him." Kent pulled the bloodied handkerchief from his nose.

Jack wanted to smash him in the face again, but instead he whirled on his heels, grabbed Marisa's hand and raced back to his car.

"What do we do now?" Marisa asked as he pulled his cell phone out of his pocket.

"I've got to call Harold. I need two million dollars from him."

"When this is all over, he'll try to take the boys from you." Marisa's voice was a tortured whisper.

"Probably," he agreed and fought a wave of fear so intense it brought a mist of tears to his eyes. "But it's a risk I have to take."

He punched in the number for his ex-father-in-law, and when Harold answered his phone Jack explained to him what had happened and what he needed from him.

When he hung up he turned to Marisa and stared at her with a hollowness he'd never felt before. It was as if he were already grieving a loss too enormous to comprehend.

Marisa must have seen something in his eyes that spoke of the depth of his despair. She placed a hand on his forearm. "Don't give up, Jack. Mick and David need you to stay strong. Patrick wants money. Once he has what he wants he'll let them go."

"I hope you're right," he said. He started the car and pulled away from Kent's. Once he had his boys back safe and sound he would see to it that Kent spent the rest of his life behind bars. Right now all he cared about were his babies.

If anything happened to his boys, then there was no place on earth that Kent or Patrick could hide. Jack would make it his mission in life to find them and destroy them.

Harold Rothchild was a handsome man. His snow-white hair was in stark contrast to the black suit he wore with a casual elegance.

He'd arrived at Jack's moments ago with two large suitcases. He'd shown no emotion when Jack had introduced Marisa as his wife.

During the time that they'd waited for him to arrive Marisa had taken a quick shower, washing off the soot and ash that had covered her. As she'd stood beneath the spray of water she'd wept with fear for Mick and David. She'd cried uncontrollably for Jack.

Jack spent the first few minutes after Harold's arrival telling the tall, lean man what had happened in the past couple hours. Harold said nothing but his piercing blue gaze never left Jack's face.

They were all seated at the dining-room table, Jack's cell phone in front of him as he waited for another call from Patrick.

"Patrick Moore." Harold frowned as he said the name. "He's a dead man and doesn't even know it yet."

With everything that had happened since Jack had pulled her from the fire, Marisa suddenly remembered what Patrick had told her about his real identity.

"His name isn't really Patrick Moore," she said. Both men turned to look at her. "I just remembered, he told me his name was Paz...Paz Martin or Martinez."

"Paz Marquez." Harold's voice was flat as he stared at Marisa.

"Yes, that's it," she replied. "He said something about a diamond and his father being murdered."

Harold leaned back in the chair, his face turning the shade of ash. "This isn't about money. It's about revenge. It's about that damned diamond." He reached a hand up and rubbed his forehead, as if a headache had suddenly made itself known.

"What are you talking about? Who is Paz Marquez?" Jack asked.

"Antonio Marquez, Paz's father, found the diamond that we now know as The Tears of the Quetzal." Some of the natural color began to return to Harold's face. "He didn't turn it over to my father like he was supposed to but rather pocketed it and quit his job. My father found out about it, and one night he met Antonio in the mine, retrieved the diamond from him, then buried him alive." He bowed his head, looking as if he carried the weight of the world on his shoulders. "I was just a kid, but I was there and saw it happen. I never told anyone, and now it appears I'm paying for my silence."

He reached up and straightened his black and silver tie, as if finding comfort in the small gesture. Marisa noticed that his hands shook slightly.

"I tried to make it right," he continued. "As soon as I was old enough I began sending money to Paz's mother, Juanita. Because of my father she was left a widow with three small children. I arranged for her to move to Arizona and start a new life. I thought it would be enough."

"Apparently it wasn't," Jack replied.

Harold offered him a tight smile. "I always thought it would be you who did something stupid and put those boys at risk. I never dreamed it would be me who brought danger to them."

"It doesn't matter now," Jack replied. "It's just

important that you and I work together to bring the boys home."

Marisa turned her head to stare out the window. The emergency equipment had been carted away, and the barn was nothing but a pile of rubble. Dusk was falling and the coming of night terrified her.

Where was David? Where was Mick? Were they afraid? Were they crying out for her?

Her heart ached with the need to have David and Mick back in her arms. In the short span of time that she'd been in their lives they had crawled so deeply into her heart that she felt as if she'd given birth to both of them.

It wasn't just thoughts of the boys that shattered her heart. As she looked across the table at Jack she wanted to weep with his pain.

He looked as if he'd been shot in the gut and couldn't staunch the bleeding. His face was an unhealthy shade of pale, and his eyes were feverish shards of pain.

The evening passed in a torturous tick of the clock. Each minute felt like an eternity as they waited for Patrick to make contact.

Marisa made sandwiches that nobody ate and coffee that they all consumed with alacrity as they waited for the call that would hopefully bring the boys home.

Home. That's what Marisa had begun to think of this place with Jack and the boys. Since their whirlwind marriage she'd been happier than she'd ever been in her life.

Even though she'd known better she'd begun to have dreams about their future. She'd fantasized about school carnivals and baseball games, about family outings and laughter. Always in those fantasies she and Jack were proud parents who not only loved the boys but also each other.

But they were just fantasies, and she knew without question that no matter what happened tonight the fantasy was coming to an end.

Even if the boys were returned safe and sound, she had a feeling that Harold would fight Jack for them, and in Jack's current frame of mind, she wasn't sure he would fight back.

The knot that filled her chest at telling them all goodbye was as painful as her gasps for breath when she'd been inside the burning barn.

It wasn't just the boys that she would miss. It was Jack. She'd known in the first five minutes of meeting him that he was the kind of man who could own her heart. She'd tried to keep herself distant from him but to no avail. He'd ingrained himself so deeply into her heart then when she finally would have to leave, she would leave a piece of herself behind with him forever.

She'd just gotten up for the coffeepot to refill their cups when Jack's cell phone rang. For a moment it was as if everyone in the room froze.

Marisa's heart beat so loudly in her head she wondered if she'd only imagined the ring of the phone. It was only when Jack leaped forward and grabbed the cell phone that she realized it really had rung.

"Cortland," he snapped.

The tension in the room was so intense it made Marisa's stomach churn. She'd grieved long and hard for a baby she'd never held, a baby who had never drawn a breath of air. She couldn't imagine grieving for Mick and David. The pain was simply too unbearable.

"I've got the money," Jack said. "I want to talk to my boys." He rose from the table with such force his chair crashed to the floor behind him. "Damn it, you put Mick on so I can talk to him."

His angry features instantly transformed to something softer. "Hey, Mick. Are you okay, buddy? Don't worry—Daddy is going to come for you, okay?"

Marisa could tell the moment Patrick got back on the phone as a hard mask of rage replaced the tenderness on Jack's face.

"Just tell me where to meet you and I'll be there with the money," Jack said. "Yeah…yeah, all right. I got it." His eyes narrowed to dangerous slits. "And, Patrick, if either of those boys has so much as a scratch then I'll kill you." He hung up the phone.

"Where?" Harold asked, his features as ferocious as Jack's.

"Eleven o'clock tonight behind the old King's Inn casino downtown," Jack replied.

"Shouldn't we go to the police?" Marisa asked, afraid that something was going to go terribly wrong. She knew the location of King's Inn. It had been a dive where some of the locals had gone to gamble, but three months ago it had been closed down.

"No, no cops," Harold said, and Jack quickly echoed the sentiment.

"But what about Kent? Shouldn't he be arrested as an accomplice?" she asked. "For all we know he's already left town."

"We'll get him," Harold replied. "He's a stupid man who would sell out a friend for the price of a six-pack of beer." He looked at Jack. "I imagine you know that it was Kent who was keeping me apprised of what was going on here with you and the boys."

"Yeah, it's amazing when you realize who you can't trust in your life," Jack said. His gaze sought Marisa's and he smiled. "And it's equally amazing when you realize who you can trust."

Rather than make her feel better, the smile shot an icy chill through Marisa. If anything happened to Mick and David she would be devastated, but she knew in her heart, in her very soul, that the man she loved would be completely destroyed.

Chapter 12

Jack drove slowly down the street toward the old King's Inn casino. The downtown area that most people visited was the Fremont Street Experience, five blocks of casinos and restaurants beneath a large barrel canopy with light shows to enthrall the crowd.

There was a seedier Las Vegas downtown, where small casinos served a desperate crowd and drug addicts lingered in the shadows. Pimps and prostitutes yelled to passing cars, and pickpockets and muggers lay in wait for an unwary out-of-towner.

It was to that area that Jack drove.

He was alone in his car with two million dollars

in cash and was hoping—praying—that Patrick had enough morality left not to harm his boys.

More than a touch of fear rode with him in the car. The terror burned in his heart that beat with enough adrenaline to fuel a football team in a championship game.

Harold had insisted that he was coming along, but Jack had refused to allow him to ride with him. Patrick had demanded that Jack come alone, and he wasn't about to break the rules of a game where Mick and David were the trophies.

It was agreed that Harold and Marisa would follow him and park a block away from the rendezvous and wait for Jack to get the kids.

Jack knew the boys would want Marisa. They would need her loving arms wrapped around them and assuring them that everything was all right. Truth be told there had been moments in the long night of waiting where Jack had needed her arms around him.

As he pulled into the deserted parking lot behind the abandoned building that had once been a casino he glanced at his watch. He was fifteen minutes early.

He parked the car and turned out his headlights, then took a quick survey of his surroundings. An old trash Dumpster sat against the back of the building, barely discernible in the darkness. Other than that there was nothing in the area.

The streetlights from in front of the building barely pierced the darkness back here. Tension screamed inside him as he glanced at his watch once again.

He rolled down his window to allow in the stifling July night air, but the heat couldn't begin to melt the icy center inside him.

He touched the butt of the revolver on the seat next to him. There was no way he'd put himself in this kind of position without bringing a weapon. He had no intention of using it unless it was to save his own life. The last thing he wanted was to try to be a hero and wind up turning a volatile situation into something worse.

As far as he was concerned Patrick could have Harold's money as long as he returned Mick and David unharmed.

Money could be replaced.

Little boys could not.

He looked at his watch once again, apprehension roiling inside him. He had no idea from which direction Patrick would come so he swiveled his head in all directions as he waited.

"Don't take them away from me," he whispered. "I've only just learned to do it all right. Don't let it all be for nothing." Jack had never been an overly religious man, but he prayed now, hoping that God heard his prayers.

He was well aware of the fact that Harold would

probably push for custody when this was all over.
Jack would fight him with every breath in his body.
In his heart, Jack truly believed that those boys
belonged with him.

And for the first time he recognized that he'd
become the man he'd finally wanted to be—the man
his parents would be proud of, the man Marisa had
known was inside him.

He straightened in his seat as a car without its headlights on slid around the building and parked facing
his. For several agonizing moments nothing happened.

A throb of tension beat at the base of Jack's
skull, and his hands grew slick with sweat on the
steering wheel.

Suddenly the car's high beams came on, half
blinding Jack.

The driver door opened and Patrick stepped out.
The headlights gleamed on the metal of the gun in
his hand. Jack grabbed the revolver from the passenger seat and opened his door as well.

As he got out of his car he smoothly shoved the
revolver into his waistband in the small of his back.
"Where are my boys?" Jack asked harshly.

"First things first," Patrick replied. "Throw your
weapon on the ground," he demanded. Jack hesitated. "Come on, Cortland, I know you wouldn't be
stupid enough to show up here unarmed. Now toss it
and we can get this over with. Slow and easy. Don't

make me get nervous. Trust me, you don't want me nervous."

There was no way Jack intended to take a chance. He didn't want to piss off Patrick. He just wanted to get his sons and walk away.

With a slow movement he reached behind him and grabbed the revolver, then bent down and placed it on the oily pavement and scooted it away with his foot. It clattered and came to rest several feet from where Jack stood.

"Where are my boys?" he asked again.

"I told you, first things first. Where's the money?"

"Two suitcases in the backseat of my car," Jack replied.

"Get them out."

Jack did as he was instructed and pulled the two heavy cases from the backseat of his car. The fact that he didn't see the boys in Patrick's car worried him. He hoped they were there, perhaps asleep in the back.

"Now, bring them halfway to me."

"First tell me where Mick and David are," Jack countered.

"They're in a safe place, and I'll tell you exactly where they are once I have the money."

"How do I know I can trust you?" Jack asked.

Patrick's teeth gleamed white as he smiled. "Well, now, I guess you really don't know."

The red wash of rage threatened to take over Jack, but he tamped it down. He'd never wanted to hurt a man so much, but he realized in this drama he was powerless to do anything but what Patrick asked of him. The stakes were too high for him to gamble in any way.

As he carried the cases forward, his heart beat so frantically he thought he might be on the verge of a heart attack. A thousand thoughts raced through his head. His heart didn't just beat frantically for himself but also for Marisa.

She'd already suffered an enormous loss in her life, and she'd loved the boys enough to give up her personal freedom, to bind her life to his in the best interest of the children. If this all went horribly wrong he recognized that he wouldn't be the only one devastated.

He dropped the suitcases where Patrick indicated. "Now step back," Patrick said. The gun remained pointed directly at Jack's chest.

As Jack backed away Patrick moved forward, his dark brown eyes gleaming with triumph, with greed. He knelt to open the first case but kept the gun focused on Jack.

"It's all there," Jack said. "Two million dollars in unmarked bills. Now give me my kids. We had nothing to do with your father's murder."

Patrick's smile fell, and raw emotion shone from his eyes. "So you know who I am."

"Marisa told me. I managed to get her out of the barn. She told me that you're Paz Marquez. Harold's father murdered yours in a mine when you were a boy. This isn't my fight, Paz, and it certainly isn't Mick and David's battle."

Paz's features twisted with rage. "He ruined my life."

"And you killed his daughter. I'd say the score is even."

"It will never be even," Paz exclaimed, the cords of his neck standing out. "Yeah, I killed Candace because I wanted the ring, the ring with the diamond that should have been mine. But Candace's murder was just the beginning. I took it upon myself to make the Rothchilds' life hell ever since I rid the world of Harold's precious little girl."

"How did you manage to evade the cops for so long?" Jack demanded.

"I was a master of disguise…and highly motivated. He smirked. "It wasn't hard to camouflage my identity when I kidnapped Jenna Rothchild and Marisa's aunt. I would have gladly killed them both if that's what it would have taken to get back the ring—but it wasn't necessary." He shrugged. "I knew Rita Perez had the ring, and I knew the easiest way to get close to her was to get close to Marisa. They made it easy for me to take the ring from Rita's apartment."

He was wired, babbling with pride but the gun never wavered in his grip.

"Harold tried to make it right," Jack said, trying to appeal to any reason Paz might possess. "He sent your mother money. He moved you to Arizona so you could have a good life."

"A good life?" Paz spat on the ground. "My mother went through money almost as quickly as she went through men. Harold even had a brief affair with her, which is how I knew that he was the one behind our sudden good fortune." He sneered. "He'd throw us a few dollars and then go back to his multimillion-dollar lifestyle. The score isn't even. It will *never* be even."

"Just give me my kids," Jack said, his voice cracking with his emotion. "You have the diamond ring, and you have the money. What else do you want from me? You want me to beg? I'll beg. For God's sake, just give my kids back to me."

Paz drew a deep breath, as if to calm the rage inside him. "I've been thinking that maybe this is just the down payment," he said.

Down payment? The implication of those words created a red fog inside Jack's brain. "Where are my boys?" he raged as he took a step toward Patrick.

"Get back or I'll shoot you," Patrick yelled as Jack took another step toward him.

Jack heard the sound of the gun, a sharp crack that echoed in his head.

There was a split second when his heart cried out. Not because he believed he was about to die, but rather because he would die without seeing Mick and David's first day of school, he'd miss seeing them become teenagers—become men.

His heart cried not just for his children but for Marisa, whom he now recognized he loved not just as the mother figure to his boys but as the woman he wanted in his life forever.

He tensed, waiting for the killing bullet, but instead he watched in stunned surprise as Patrick crumpled to the ground.

Harold stepped out from around the side of the building, a gun in his hand. "I couldn't let him kill you," he said.

Jack stared at the unmoving Paz with a growing sense of alarm. "Oh, God, what have you done?" Jack raced to the fallen man, vaguely aware that Marisa had joined Harold.

It took only one look to see that Paz was dead. Jack stared down at him with a growing sense of horror. He finally looked at Harold and Marisa. "He didn't tell me where the boys were. I don't know where Mick and David are." His voice cracked once again.

A cry escaped Marisa, and she ran to Paz's car and tore open the back door. "They aren't in here." She began to cry.

"I had to shoot him. Otherwise he would have killed you," Harold said, his voice a mix of anger and fear.

The trunk. Jack stared at the car with a new sense of horror. Was it possible that Paz had put his sons into the trunk of his car?

He leaned down and fumbled in Paz's pockets until he found the car keys. As he approached the trunk the only sound was that of Marisa's sobs.

A roar resounded in his head. Would he open the trunk lid and find them curled up together, not breathing? His hand shook so violently that it took him three stabs before he managed to get the key into the lock.

He opened the trunk and wasn't sure whether to be relieved or devastated. The trunk was empty. "Call the police," he said, his voice sounding as if it came from very far away. Where were his sons? Where in the hell had Paz stashed them?

They were all seated around a large interrogation table in the Las Vegas Metropolitan Police Department. Kent had been picked up and now sat in shackles next to Officer Jeff Cookson, who was trying to make sense of a dead body behind a deserted casino and one of the wealthiest men in the country seated next to him.

Marisa and Jack sat side by side, their hands clasped in a tight grip as they listened to Cookson grill Kent for any clues that might help them locate Mick and David.

An Amber Alert had been issued but so far had

yielded nothing. Officers were out searching the area around the King's Inn casino. It was the middle of the night and David and Mick were out there someplace, alone and hopefully still alive.

Marisa felt Jack's desperation radiating through his hand. It was a desperation she shared.

"I met Patrick in a bar," Kent now said. "We got to drinking and talking, and it wasn't long before he told me how much he hated the Rothchilds and I told him how much I hated Jack."

Kent looked at Jack with narrowed eyes. "We were best friends. You could have changed my life, but you left here and never looked back."

"You could have changed your own life, Kent," Jack replied with a rough edge to his voice. "I was never responsible for you."

They had already learned that it had been Kent who had tried to break in to the ranch. He'd watched the house and had known that Marisa and Jack often stayed up late in the living room talking.

The plan had been for Kent to break in to Marisa's bedroom and steal silently across the hallway to the boys' room. If they'd awakened they wouldn't have been afraid to see Kent. Patrick had been waiting just outside the window of that room to get the boys from Kent.

When that particular plan hadn't worked, Patrick had decided to take care of getting the boys on his own. When Jack had called Kent to make arrangements to meet at Kent's house and talk about their fight, Kent had called Patrick to let him know Marisa and the boys would be alone at the ranch.

As Marisa had listened to him talking about the plot her blood had chilled, something she hadn't thought possible, as her blood was already cold enough to freeze her solid.

What had Patrick done with the boys? Where could he have put them while he went to retrieve his ransom? Were they warm enough? Were they thirsty or hungry? Were they still alive?

Her heart lurched, and she shoved that particular thought away. She had to believe that they were all right. Any thought to the contrary was too difficult to fathom.

"I've told you a million times, I don't know what he did with the boys," Kent exclaimed. "I don't know where he was living or what his exact plan was. We only met in bars or at my place. This isn't my fault. I didn't know he was dangerous."

Marisa stared at Kent in incomprehension. How could he have done this? Even if he'd hated Jack how could he have placed those two little boys in harm's way?

Jack leaned across the table, his stormy gray eyes swirling with fury. "You didn't do anything to change your life in the past, but you've definitely done something to change your future. I'll make sure you stay locked up for the rest of your miserable life."

Jack unclasped Marisa's hand, stood and stalked out of the room. Marisa went after him, and she found him leaning against the wall outside the interrogation room.

Deep sobs wrenched his body, and Marisa wrapped her arms around him and held tight. Together they wept for the lost boys, their fear palpable in the air around them.

Marisa had no idea how much time had passed before he finally straightened, leaned back against the wall and raised a hand to shield his eyes as if embarrassed by his show of emotion.

"I'm trying to be strong," he finally said, his voice weary.

"You are strong, Jack." She reached up and grabbed his hand and looked into his eyes. "It's a courageous man who walks into a deserted back lot with two suitcases full of money. It's a selfless man who goes to the person he fears most to get the money to save his boys, and it's a strong man who faces up to his fear for his children."

"Where are they, Marisa? What could he have done with them?" The torment in his eyes reflected the emotion inside her heart.

"I wish I knew." Once again he reached for her and they stood in an embrace until Officer Cookson and Harold came out of the interrogation room.

"I don't think he has any information that can help us find your kids," he said. "He's been taken

back to the jail, and he'll be charged first thing
Monday morning. In the meantime I need to see
what we're going to do with Mr. Rothchild."

Harold said nothing. In the past hour he'd looked
as if he'd aged ten years. His skin held an unhealthy
pallor, and his posture was that of a defeated man.

"He saved my life," Jack said. "If he hadn't shot
Paz, then I wouldn't be here right now. You can't
arrest him—he killed a dangerous man."

"We're going now to meet with the district
attorney and explain the whole situation to him. It's
doubtful that Mr. Rothchild will face any charges,"
Cookson said.

Before any of them could move from their position another officer appeared. "Hey, thought you
might be interested that we just got a call from the
Timberline Motel. The manager called to tell us he'd
found a toddler wandering around in the parking
lot. He's got the kid in the office and is waiting for
somebody to respond."

Jack grabbed Marisa's hand so tight she winced
beneath the pressure. "The Timberline Motel?
Where is it?" he asked.

"Let's go," Cookson said. "You can follow me."

Within minutes Marisa was in the passenger seat
of Jack's car and Harold was in the back as they
barreled down the street just behind Cookson's patrol
car.

Marisa's heart beat frantically, although she was

afraid to acknowledge the tiny ray of hope that tried to emerge. It could be the child of somebody staying at the motel. It might have nothing to do with David or Mick.

Jack's knuckles were white on the steering wheel and a muscle knotted in his jaw. She wanted to tell him not to hope too much, but she saw it shining from his eyes—the need to believe that the child in the parking lot of the motel was one of his own. And even though she was afraid for him, she didn't want to be the one to take that hope away.

The Timberline Motel was located in the downtown area about ten minutes from the abandoned casino behind which Paz had been killed.

In the land of flashing, gaudy lights the one-story building was woefully inadequate, as the vacancy sign sported more than a dozen burned-out bulbs. It was obviously a low-rent operation, the kind of motel that probably rented out more by the hour than by the night.

Jack's car squealed to a halt in front of the office, and all three of them jumped out of the car and raced toward the office door.

Marisa was just behind Jack as he burst through the door. She cried out in sweet relief as she saw both David and Mick sitting on chairs in the small lobby.

"Daddy!" Mick cried, and met Jack halfway. Jack released a deep sob as he grabbed Mick to him, then rushed to David and picked him up in his arms, as well.

"Daddy, David needs time-out. He went out the window again," Mick exclaimed with a hint of indignity.

"Time-out," David said and nodded his head with a happy smile.

"We'll worry about time-out later," Jack replied through his tears.

Little David had pulled his Houdini act, climbing out the window of whatever room they had been in. Marisa gave Jack a moment to hug and kiss them, then she moved forward, needing those little-boy hugs and kisses for herself.

As the four of them had a group hug, Officer Cookson and Harold questioned the manager of the motel. "Room 121. He checked in as Martin Bale," Cookson said to Jack. "He didn't show identification and paid cash for one night. I've called in the crime-scene unit to check it all out."

"I'm taking my boys home," Jack said. He held Mick in his arms, and Marisa hugged tight to David, reveling in the warmth of his little arms around her.

"I'm sure we'll have more questions for you," Officer Cookson protested.

"Not tonight," Jack said firmly. "It's way past my boys' bedtime. I'm taking them home now so they can sleep in their own beds." He looked unflinching at the officer. "If you have any questions for me you can come to the ranch either tonight or in the morning, but right now we're going home."

"I'll stay here," Harold said. "I can tell them whatever they need to know, and then Officer Cookson can take me back to my car."

As they walked out of the motel office, a euphoric joy flowed through Marisa's heart. It was over. The danger, the drama, the terror, it was all over now and her family was safe and sound.

Her family. A fierce protectiveness surged through her. Mick and David and Jack. In a shockingly short period of time they had become her heart, her very soul. They were a unit of love she couldn't imagine not having in her life.

They had just buckled the boys into their car seats when Harold walked toward them. Instantly Marisa tensed.

In the minutes that they had driven together and followed Jack to the back lot of the King's Inn casino, Harold had talked a lot, and in that conversation Marisa had recognized him as a man who admitted the mistakes he'd made in his life, a man who had sounded as if he wanted to make amends, turn things around.

But as he approached their car every protective urge she had inside her rose to the surface. She couldn't forget that Harold was the one person on earth who could possibly take the boys from Jack.

"Jack," he called. "We need to talk."

She stepped between Jack and Harold. "Mr. Rothchild, it's late and we need to get the boys home where they belong." She emphasized the last words. "Surely whatever you have to say can wait for another day."

To her surprise Harold's mouth turned upward in a half smile. "You're a pushy little thing, aren't you? I can see what Jack sees in you. I think Jack will want to hear what I have to say."

Jack placed a hand on Marisa's shoulder and faced his father-in-law. "What is it, Harold?"

"I've made a lot of mistakes in my life, Jack. I haven't always been a good man, a righteous man."

"You came all the way out here to tell me that?" Jack asked dryly.

Harold shook his head. "I came all the way out here to tell you that I see now that taking those boys from you would be just another mistake for me. I won't fight you for custody," he said. "I see how those boys love you…how you love them. I just wanted you to know that I have no intention of causing you problems." He looked him straight in the eye. "I promise you that you don't have to worry about me anymore. I might be a lot of things, but you know that I'm a man of my word."

He held out his hand to Jack. Marisa released a tremulous sigh. She believed Harold and apparently so did Jack, for he grasped Harold's hand and they shook.

Marisa felt it in the air, the healing between the two men who both only wanted what was best for the precious little boys who were already sound asleep in their car seats.

"If you need anything for them or for yourself, you call me and I'll see that you get it," Harold said as the handshake ended.

It was only when they were in the car and headed home that the full significance of Harold's words hit Marisa and all the joy she'd felt minutes before whooshed out of her.

Jack now understood what the boys needed from him, both as a disciplinarian and as a loving parent. Harold had promised he had no intention of fighting Jack for custody.

That meant her role in Jack's life was now unnecessary. The very reason for their marriage no longer existed. She was no longer needed. She glanced over at Jack and wondered just how long it would take before he came to the same conclusion.

Chapter 13

Jack sat in the boys' room for hours after they'd come home from the police station. He'd needed to be close enough to them to hear them breathing, to smell the familiar scent of them.

When he thought of how close he'd come to losing them, his heart ached and the memory of his terror nearly froze him in place. So close—so frighteningly close.

They were safe and home where they belonged, and Harold had promised that he wouldn't try to take them away.

Jack believed him. As Harold had said, he might be many things but as he'd reminded Jack he was also a man of his word. He would cause no more anxiety as far as the boys were concerned. Jack could sleep nights knowing that Harold was no longer a threat.

It had to have been the love that Harold saw that existed among the four of them, the family unity that they'd shown must have been what had made him come to his decision to leave them alone.

Sure, there would probably be times in the future where Jack and Harold would butt heads, and certainly Jack expected Harold to be a part of the boys' lives. But the fear of losing them had eased out of Jack's heart, leaving nothing but his intense love behind.

It was near dawn when Marisa appeared in the doorway. She was clad in her little red nightgown and her long hair was tousled around her head—the very sight of her chased any memory of the terror away and he finally rose from the chair and left the boys' room.

"You need to get some sleep," she said softly.

He raked a hand through his hair and released a weary sigh. "Yeah." He smiled and reached out and traced his finger down the side of her cheek, the warmth of her skin stirring him. "Come to bed with me?"

There was a moment of hesitation as she gazed up at him. "All right," she said.

Together they walked down the hallway to his

bedroom. He stripped off his clothes as she crawled in under the sheets.

He was exhausted, both physically and emotionally, but the minute he got into bed next to her and drew her warm body against his, he wanted her.

He didn't want to talk. He didn't want to hash over what the night had held. He just wanted to make love to his wife.

She seemed to sense what he needed. She pulled off her gown and tossed it over the side of the bed, and they came together with a tenderness that was healing.

The horror of the night fell away, replaced by the heat of her lips and the comfort of her naked body against his.

There was a sense of desperation in her kiss, in the way her hands clutched his shoulders, and he guessed that she was chasing away the demons that had plagued them through the long night.

He held her tight and kissed her with all the passion, all the love that burned in his heart. This was the woman he'd been meant to marry, the woman who completed him like no other.

The winds of fate had blown her into his life. She'd needed his boys and they had needed her. The fact that Jack had fallen so deeply in love with her was just icing on the cake.

As he caressed her she cried out softly in pleasure. He loved the feel of her silky flesh, the taste of her skin as he ran his lips from one breast to the other.

He'd never felt this way with Candace. He'd never felt this need, this connection that went far beyond the physical. When he knew she was ready he moved to take her completely.

He entered her and looked down at her, her face bathed in the dawn light. Tears oozed from the corners of her eyes, tears he assumed were of relief, of pleasure.

He closed his eyes as the sweet sensations of being joined with her swept over him. He was lost in her, and being with her chased the last of the horror away, leaving him sated and at peace.

The sound of the boys awoke them just after eight. Jack released a small groan and tried to pull Marisa closer against him, but she quickly slid out of bed and pulled her nightgown over her head.

"Get some more sleep," she said. "I'll take care of them."

Jack closed his eyes as she left the room. Minutes later he heard the sound of Mick's and David's laughter, and there was no way he could stay in bed.

He wanted to be a part of that merriment. He needed to be surrounded by Mick and David and Marisa. His family, he thought with a proud, protective surge.

He got out of bed and pulled on a pair of jeans, then left the room to join the love and laughter.

* * *

"Harold won't face any charges," Rita told Jack and Marisa as they sat in the living room. She had arrived at the ranch just after lunch to check in on her niece and see how everyone was doing.

"I didn't figure he would," Jack replied. "Sure you don't want some coffee or anything?"

"Thanks, but no, I'm fine. Besides, I can only stay a few minutes. We're still sorting through this whole mess." She looked over to where Mick and David sat on the floor with their trucks. "We found some child liquid pain medication in the room. We believe Paz tried to drug the boys before he left them alone last night, but apparently he didn't give them enough to keep them asleep."

"Thank God," Jack said.

"Mick told me they had hamburgers and a drink, then he and David fell asleep on the bed," Marisa said. "They woke up sometime later and they were alone. That's when David decided it would be more fun outside the room. He couldn't manage to twist the door lock, but he could climb up on the dresser just below the window."

"This is one time I'm glad he has a fascination with going out windows," Jack exclaimed.

He gazed at his sons, his heart filling with joy. His gaze shifted to look at Marisa. She'd been quiet this morning, distant and withdrawn since the moment she'd gotten out of bed.

"If Harold hadn't killed Paz, then Paz would have spent the rest of his life behind bars. We know he killed Candace, and we have DNA evidence from Jenna Rothchild's kidnapping that will probably tie him to that, as well." Rita raised a hand to the bandage on the side of her head. "He came way too close to killing me, and it still scares me to think that Marisa might have died in that fire."

Marisa reached out and grabbed her aunt's hand. "Thank God that didn't happen."

"The good news is we located a deposit box in a bank where Paz had placed The Tears of the Quetzal. The ring is now back in police custody where it belongs," Rita said.

"And you still have your job," Marisa said teasingly. Rita had explained to them about the missing ring and how desperate she'd been to find it.

Rita grinned. "Thank goodness my supervisor has a heart. And I've promised that I'll never check out any evidence and bring it home again."

"So all's well that ends well," Jack said.

"We still don't know the extent of Paz's crimes. It might take us some time to unravel it all," Rita said.

"His hatred had years to fester," Marisa said.

"Like Kent's did." Jack frowned as he thought of the man who had once been his friend. "He was too afraid to leave here and take off on his own, too afraid to risk Los Angeles, but he hated me for having the courage to do it without him."

"He'll have a lot of time to think about it in prison," Rita said.

The three talked for a few more minutes, then Rita stood to leave. "Marisa, will you walk me out?"

Jack said goodbye to the FBI agent, then watched as Rita and Marisa left the house together. He got down on the floor between Mick and David and began to play with them.

Now perhaps they could all go back to the life they'd been living before the kidnapping. He wanted that. He wanted the comfortable routine. He wanted the boys and laughter in the daytime and Marisa and passion at night.

For the first time in forever, Jack saw his future before him and he liked what he saw, was eager to live his life—a life filled with love.

Marisa came back inside and went directly to her bedroom. Jack frowned. Her mood was making him uneasy. What was going on in her head? Today should be a day of joy, but a sense of sadness clung to Marisa, a sadness Jack didn't understand and one that worried him more than a little bit.

He thought of the tears he'd seen in her eyes when they'd made love. He'd believed at the time that they had been tears of joy, of relief after the trauma they had suffered. Had he been wrong?

His worry increased when she poked her head out

of her room and called to him. "Jack, could I speak to you for a minute?" she asked.

"I'll be right back, boys," he said as he pulled himself off the floor.

"Hurry up, Daddy. We're going to have a truck race," Mick exclaimed.

As always the word *daddy* shot sweet warmth through him. Bad Jack was gone. Even when he reprimanded them now, they still called him Daddy. Marisa had given him back his fatherhood.

Jack stepped into the guest room, which smelled like her perfume. "What's up?" he asked.

"Aunt Rita brought me something that I thought you'd want to have." She held out a white envelope toward him.

He frowned. "What's that?"

"It's the results of a paternity test for you and the boys."

He looked at her in confusion. "I didn't take a paternity test."

A flash of guilt sparked in her dark brown eyes. "I took swabs from inside the boys' mouths and a coffee cup that you had used and took them to Rita. I know it wasn't my place to do it, but I also knew that paternity was a threat that Harold was holding over your head. Anyway, Rita called in a couple of favors and got it done immediately at the FBI lab."

Jack stared at the envelope as if it were a poisonous snake. He thought of all the times Candace had hinted that she'd been unfaithful, all the times Harold had told him that there was a strong possibility that at least one of the boys wasn't his.

"It doesn't matter," he finally said. He shoved his hands into his pockets. "It doesn't matter what's written on that paper. Both those boys are mine. They're my heart, and a stupid test isn't going to change that."

"Open it, Jack. Go on. It will put an end to the question." She held the envelope closer to him.

Reluctantly he pulled his hands from his pockets and reached out for the envelope. The paper felt hot between his fingers. His mouth went dry as his heart began to beat a quickened rhythm.

He'd told her the truth. It didn't matter to him what the test revealed. Both David and Mick were his sons in every way that counted. Whether or not his blood ran through their veins wouldn't change his love for them.

Still, in knowledge was power. Even though Harold had promised not to try to take the boys, there might come a time when paternity became an issue. Wasn't it better he be armed with the truth now?

His fingers felt big and clumsy as he fumbled to open the envelope. He pulled out the paper inside and allowed the envelope to flutter to the floor at his feet.

"Go on, Jack. Look at it," Marisa said softly. Her

eyes shone overly bright and what he wanted to do was throw the paper on the floor and take her to bed. Instead he opened it and looked.

He released a small cry as he read that in the case of both boys he was their father. There was absolutely no question about it. He looked up to see Marisa's smile. "You knew," he said softly.

She nodded. "I read it before I gave it to you."

"What would you have done if the results had been different? Would you have still given it to me?"

She frowned thoughtfully. "I'm not sure. Thank goodness I didn't have to face that particular dilemma."

It was only then that Jack glanced over her shoulder and saw her suitcase open on the bed. "What are you doing?" he asked.

The smile that had lifted the corners of her luscious mouth fell and her eyes darkened. "I'm packing."

"Packing?" He looked at her in bewilderment. "Where are we going?"

"Not we—me." She averted her gaze from his and took a step backward. "You don't need me here anymore, Jack. You're doing fine with the boys, and Harold has promised he won't fight you for custody. There's really no reason for me to stay here."

A million thoughts flew through Jack's head, a million reasons that he wanted her to stay. "The boys need you," he said.

"They have all they need in you," she replied, her gaze still not meeting his.

She walked over to the closet, pulled several blouses from their hangers and laid them on the bed next to her suitcase.

A crazy sense of panic filled him. It wasn't alarm over the fact that when she left he'd have nobody to help him with Mick and David. He knew she was right. He'd be fine alone with the boys—he just didn't want to be.

The panic came from the fact that he needed her, that he loved her, but it wasn't fair for him to put that on her. She'd made it clear from the very beginning that she was here for his boys, not for him.

"I wish you'd reconsider." His words were woefully inadequate for the pain that filled his heart.

She shook her head. "It's for the best." She walked back to stand in front of him and pulled off the ring he'd given her when they'd exchanged their vows. "This is yours. I just had it out on loan."

He shoved his hands back into his pockets, unwilling to take the ring that had once belonged to his mother and now in his mind belonged to Marisa.

She shrugged and placed the ring on the top of the dresser, where the sunlight sparkled on the little diamond. "I would prefer you not tell the boys I'm leaving for good. I'll tell them I'm taking a little trip. They're young. In a couple of weeks they will forget all about me." Her voice cracked slightly.

As she began to fold the blouses and place them in her suitcase Mick yelled and Jack left her bedroom to tend to the boys.

He knew how to make music. He knew now what to do when one of the boys misbehaved. But he didn't know how to stop the woman he loved from walking away from him.

Hot tears pressed at Marisa's eyes as she sat on the edge of the bed. She tried to staunch them, but they came without volition, fast and furiously running down her cheeks.

She'd awakened that morning with the warmth of Jack's arms around her, with the scent of him lingering on her skin, and she'd known she had to leave.

It would be less painful now than it would be later. At least she was leaving of her own volition rather than being asked to leave by Jack.

Still, that didn't ease the pain that crashed through her. She'd thought she could do this. She'd believed she could marry Jack for the best interest of the boys and keep herself emotionally distant from Jack.

She'd been wrong. Jack had stirred a love and passion in her far greater than she'd ever felt before and it terrified her.

Eventually he wouldn't be satisfied being married to a woman he'd wed only in an attempt to assure his continued custody of his sons. It was better she leave now than wait until Jack's unhappiness forced her out.

She couldn't stay here knowing she had Jack's respect, his gratitude and occasionally his desire without his love. It was just too difficult.

It would have been easier to sneak out like a thief in the night without telling any of them goodbye, but she hadn't been able to stand the thought of not getting goodbye kisses and hugs.

She pulled herself up from the bed and continued her packing. She tried to ignore the noise of the boys playing in the living room, the deep melodious sound of Jack's voice as he spoke to them.

As she finished her packing she realized there had been a small part of her that had expected this moment to come. It was why she hadn't done anything about selling her house.

All too quickly she had her bags packed and was ready to leave. Once again tears pressed hot against her eyes. She didn't want to leave and yet the depth of her emotions for Jack made her want to run, to hide, before the pain got any greater.

With a weariness that weighed heavy she stood and grabbed the suitcase that she'd initially arrived with. It felt heavier than it had when she'd carried it into the house, and she knew the additional weight was the emotion she'd packed inside as she prepared to leave.

When she went into the living room Jack and the boys were in the middle of the floor, a toy truck rally taking place before them.

"M'ssa, watch!" David said as he ran a truck over a pillow and up Jack's arm. Those familiar words nearly broke her. But she refused to weep in front of the boys.

"David, Mick, come sit here with me for a minute." She sat on the sofa and patted either side of her. The boys clambered up beside her, and she put her arms around them.

The pain that cascaded through her was unbearable. For a moment she couldn't breathe. These were the children she was supposed to have, and the man seated on the floor in front of them was the man who would forever own her heart.

"I have to go away for a little while," she finally said. "I want you to be good boys for your daddy while I'm gone."

Mick stared at her. "You promised," he said, his little features screwed up in outrage. "You promised you wouldn't go anywhere."

"Yeah, you promised," David echoed. "Bad M'ssa."

She didn't know whether to laugh or to cry. She looked at Jack, but he offered her no support. He remained on the floor, his gray eyes slightly accusing.

"I know," she said. "But you don't need me

anymore. You have your daddy, who is going to take care of you forever."

"But we want you, too," Mick said.

David leaned into Marisa with his sturdy little body and eyed her angrily. "Bad M'ssa," he repeated.

They were breaking her heart. She couldn't stop the tears that escaped, and she looked at Jack for support. "Bad M'ssa," he said.

She got up from the sofa, knowing if she didn't go now she never would. The two little boys were bad enough, but the pained look in Jack's eyes was killing her.

"I'll see you soon," she said to Mick and David. She grabbed her suitcase and started for the door, which had blurred with a new mist of tears.

"Marisa, wait."

Jack got up from the floor and walked over to her. "Boys, see if you can use those blocks and build a road."

As the two went back to their play, Jack took her by the shoulders. His mesmerizing gray eyes held hers, and again her heartbreak shuddered through her.

"I can't let you leave here without telling you something," he said.

She closed her eyes for a moment, unable to look into his eyes as he told her once again how much he appreciated what she'd done here for him and his sons.

"Marisa, I love you."

Her eyes flew open, and she stared at him in stunned surprise. "I wasn't going to say anything," he continued, "because I know that loving me had nothing to do with what you've been doing here."

"You're just grateful to me," she said as thick emotion pressed hard against her chest.

"You're right, I am grateful. But that's just the beginning of what I feel for you. I love you." He reached up and placed his palm on her cheek. "You excite me, Marisa. You inspire me. I want you to be the woman who is standing beside me as the boys grow from rambunctious little boys into fine young men…and I want us to spend the rest of our lives together."

He dropped his hand from her cheek, and his eyes darkened as if in anticipation of pain. "But I don't want you to stay here because of the boys. I want it to be because you love me, and I'll understand if you have to walk away."

"Oh, Jack, I was leaving because I'm in love with you, because I couldn't stand the idea of staying here with just your gratitude." She smiled through her tears. "I love you, Jack Cortland, and I would be honored to be the woman standing next to you for the rest of our lives."

She barely got the words out of her mouth before he took possession of her lips in a kiss that broke through any fear that might have lingered in her heart, one that electrified her with passion and with the promise of a love to last a lifetime.

"Get Mommy and Daddy," Mick yelled, and grabbed Jack around the knees. Jack toppled to the floor, and pulled Marisa along with him and there was laughter and tickles and love and Marisa knew that this was where she belonged forever...with the family of her heart.

Epilogue

People milled around the front yard, where tables heavy with food stood next to a three-piece band that filled the air with good old country music.

It had been two weeks since the kidnapping, and Jack and Marisa had decided a party was in order to celebrate their life together. They had invited all the Rothchilds as well as Marisa's family.

The party had begun an hour before and was in full swing as Marisa stood on the front porch and surveyed the scene.

Her parents stood next to Harold and his second wife, Anna. The four of them chatted with animation. Probably discussing Las Vegas real estate and the current depressed situation in the market.

Harold had gone home from the police station the morning after the kidnapping and had told his trophy wife he wanted a divorce. She'd moved out with their son, and she and Harold were now hammering out the details of the breakup. In the meantime Harold had been seeing a lot of his previous wife, Anna.

Conner Rothchild, Harold's nephew, had arrived with his new wife, Vera LaRue, a sweet, sassy woman who had worked as a dancer, and standing near the food table was Natalie, Candace's twin sister, and Natalie's new husband, Matt.

"I've got more beans ready to go out," Betty said from the doorway behind Marisa. "You know the rules, I cook—but I don't serve."

Marisa smiled at Betty. "Thanks, I'll be right in to get them." Betty had worked for the past two days fixing food for this event without a complaint. She'd even begun to allow Marisa to have her morning coffee in the kitchen, and the two women had become friends.

Jenna Rothchild and her fiancé, FBI agent Lex Duncan, stood with Rita, and Marisa could only guess that they were hashing over the subject of Paz Marquez and his numerous crimes.

She went into the kitchen and grabbed the large pan of baked beans that Betty had ready to go out on the food table.

As she carried it out she saw Sam and Max standing

awkwardly together a small distance from the crowd. They no longer made her nervous. She'd come to realize that they were painfully shy. She motioned them closer as she placed the bean pan on the table.

"I hope you two plan on getting something to eat," she said. "And maybe later you'll show me how to two-step to this music."

Sam's cheeks turned a hot pink. "I don't dance, but I definitely eat."

"I might do a little two-stepping later," Max said, his gaze going to a cute blonde named Suzie who had come as a guest of one of the others.

A hand fell on Marisa's shoulder, and she turned to see Rita. "Nice party," Rita said.

"Thanks. It's nice to see all the Rothchilds playing nice together," Marisa replied.

"Did Harold tell you he got the ring back? It's now in a warehouse waiting to be catalogued. He's donated it to his touring collection of art."

"I say good riddance. That ring caused far more heartache than good," Marisa replied.

"Oh, I don't know about that. If you believe the Mayan legend, then anyone who comes into contact with the ring finds their true love."

Marisa laughed. "I think I proved the legend wrong. I was close to the ring when Patrick and I were together, but it definitely didn't work on me where he was concerned."

Rita smiled. "You must have had some of the

ring magic on you when you met Jack. From what you've told me it was love at first sight for the both of you." Rita pulled Marisa into a hug. "I've never seen you look so happy."

"I've never been so happy," Marisa said as Rita released her.

"And I hear you've started interviewing for nannies for your agency."

Marisa nodded. "I had my first interview yesterday. Within two months I hope to have the business up and running."

"Good for you," Rita exclaimed. "And now I'm going to get a plate of this delicious food."

As Marisa headed back to the front porch she noticed Anna's daughter, Silver Rothchild, in one of the lawn chairs, her handsome husband, Captain Austin Dearing, at her side.

As Marisa watched the two, Austin smiled and reached out and touched Silver's protruding stomach. It was an intimate touch between a man and the pregnant woman he loved, and it sent just a tiny wave of pain through Marisa.

She would never know the touch of a man on her pregnant tummy. She'd never experience morning sickness or the flutter of life inside her.

The pain quickly vanished as she heard David's laughter riding the hot breeze. She looked beyond the scorched ground where the barn once had stood, out to the stables in the distance.

Jack had surprised the boys with ponies, and he was now leading them on their first pony ride. Her heart filled her chest as she gazed at the man who hadn't rocked her feet with the rhythm of his drums but had definitely rocked her world with his love.

"He's become quite a man." Harold's deep voice spoke from just behind her.

Marisa smiled at the dapper older man. "Yes, he has. He's always been a good man. He just needed someone to believe in him."

"And you do."

"With all my heart," Marisa replied.

Harold's gaze swept the area and came to rest on Anna. "It's important to have somebody in your life who believes in you, somebody who loves you. I'm hoping this time I'll get it right. Anna is a good woman."

He frowned as a cell phone rang from his pocket. He pulled it out and answered. His face turned ashen, and he held the phone away from his ear and stared at Marisa. "It's June," he said, his voice a stunned whisper.

"June?" Marisa knew that was Harold's first wife. "But I thought she was dead."

"So did I," Harold ground out. He placed the phone back to his ear and wandered away.

Marisa watched him go, wondering what new drama was about to hit the lives of the Rothchilds. She returned her gaze toward the stables and saw Jack motion to her.

Her heart filled her chest as even with the distance she could feel his love reaching out to her. It would probably be rude for her to abandon their guests and run down to the stables.

She hesitated only a moment and then took off at a quick pace toward Jack and the boys. Surely everyone would recognize that she was hurrying toward the little boys who were the sons of her heart. Surely her guests would forgive her for leaving them to run toward the man she adored and the future that shone bright with the promise of laughter and love.

* * * * *

HARLEQUIN
60 YEARS
of pure reading pleasure

We'll be spotlighting a different series
every month throughout 2009
to celebrate our 60th anniversary.

Look for Silhouette® Nocturne™ in October!

Travel through time to experience tales
that reach the boundaries of life and death.
Bestselling authors Lindsay McKenna, Cindy
Dees, P.C. Cast and Merline Lovelace join
together in a brand-new, four-book
Time Raiders miniseries.

TIME RAIDERS

August—*The Seeker*
by *USA TODAY* bestselling author Lindsay McKenna

September—*The Slayer* by Cindy Dees

October—*The Avenger*
by *New York Times* bestselling author and
coauthor of the House of Night novels P.C. Cast

November—*The Protector*
by *USA TODAY* bestselling author Merline Lovelace

Available wherever books are sold.

You're invited to join our Tell Harlequin Reader Panel!

By joining our new reader panel you will:

• Receive Harlequin® books—they are FREE and yours to keep with no obligation to purchase anything!
• Participate in fun online surveys
• Exchange opinions and ideas with women just like you
• Have a say in our new book ideas and help us publish the best in women's fiction

In addition, you will have a chance to win great prizes and receive special gifts!
See Web site for details. Some conditions apply.
Space is limited.

To join, visit us at
www.TellHarlequin.com.

In 2009 Harlequin celebrates
60 years of pure reading pleasure!

We're marking this occasion by offering
16 **FREE** full books to download and read.

Visit

www.HarlequinCelebrates.com

to choose from a variety of
great romance stories
that are absolutely **FREE!**

(Total approximate retail value of $60)

We invite you to visit and share the Web site
with your friends, family
and anyone who enjoys reading.

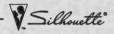

SPECIAL EDITION

FROM *NEW YORK TIMES*
BESTSELLING AUTHOR

SUSAN MALLERY

DESERT
ROGUES

THE SHEIK AND THE BOUGHT BRIDE

Victoria McCallan works in Prince Kateb's palace.
When Victoria's gambling father is caught cheating
at cards with the prince, Victoria saves her father from
going to jail by being Kateb's mistress for six months.
But the darkly handsome desert sheik isn't as harsh as
Victoria thinks he is, and Kateb finds himself attracted to
his new mistress. But Kateb has already loved and lost
once—is he willing to give love another try?

Available in October wherever books are sold.

SSE65481

REQUEST YOUR FREE BOOKS!

2 FREE NOVELS PLUS 2 FREE GIFTS!

Silhouette® Romantic

SUSPENSE

Sparked by Danger, Fueled by Passion!

YES! Please send me 2 FREE Silhouette® Romantic Suspense novels and my 2 FREE gifts (gifts are worth about $10). After receiving them, if I don't wish to receive any more books, I can return the shipping statement marked "cancel." If I don't cancel, I will receive 4 brand-new novels every month and be billed just $4.24 per book in the U.S. or $4.99 per book in Canada. That's a savings of at least 15% off the cover price! It's quite a bargain! Shipping and handling is just 50¢ per book*. I understand that accepting the 2 books and gifts places me under no obligation to buy anything. I can always return a shipment and cancel at any time. Even if I never buy another book from Silhouette, the two free books and gifts are mine to keep forever.

240 SDN EYL4   340 SDN EYMG

Name	(PLEASE PRINT)	
Address		Apt. #
City	State/Prov.	Zip/Postal Code

Signature (if under 18, a parent or guardian must sign)

Mail to the Silhouette Reader Service:
IN U.S.A.: P.O. Box 1867, Buffalo, NY 14240-1867
IN CANADA: P.O. Box 609, Fort Erie, Ontario L2A 5X3

Not valid to current subscribers of Silhouette Romantic Suspense books.

Want to try two free books from another line?
Call 1-800-873-8635 or visit www.morefreebooks.com.

* Terms and prices subject to change without notice. Prices do not include applicable taxes. Sales tax applicable in N.Y. Canadian residents will be charged applicable provincial taxes and GST. Offer not valid in Quebec. This offer is limited to one order per household. All orders subject to approval. Credit or debit balances in a customer's account(s) may be offset by any other outstanding balance owed by or to the customer. Please allow 4 to 6 weeks for delivery. Offer available while quantities last.

Your Privacy: Silhouette is committed to protecting your privacy. Our Privacy Policy is available online at www.eHarlequin.com or upon request from the Reader Service. From time to time we make our lists of customers available to reputable third parties who may have a product or service of interest to you. If you would prefer we not share your name and address, please check here. ☐

SRS09R

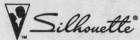

Silhouette® Romantic SUSPENSE

**Sparked by Danger,
Fueled by Passion.**

The Agent's Secret Baby

by *USA TODAY* bestselling author

Marie Ferrarella

TOP SECRET DELIVERIES

Dr. Eve Walters suddenly finds herself pregnant
after a regrettable one-night stand and turns to an
online chat room for support. She eventually learns
the true identity of her one-night stand: a DEA agent
with a deadly secret. Adam Serrano does not want
this baby or a relationship, but can fear for Eve's
and the baby's lives convince him that this is what
he has been searching for after all?

Available October wherever books are sold.

**Look for upcoming titles in
the TOP SECRET DELIVERIES miniseries**

The Cowboy's Secret Twins by Carla Cassidy—November
The Soldier's Secret Daughter by Cindy Dees—December

Visit Silhouette Books at www.eHarlequin.com

Romantic
SUSPENSE

COMING NEXT MONTH

Available September 29, 2009

#1579 PASSION TO DIE FOR—Marilyn Pappano
It's Halloween in Copper Lake, and someone's playing tricks. When Ellie
Chase's estranged mother is murdered, all the evidence points to her.
Ex-boyfriend and detective Tommy Maricci believes she's innocent, and
will do anything to prove it. But Ellie has secrets in her past, and she can't
remember what she did that night. Could she be guilty?

#1580 THE AGENT'S SECRET BABY—Marie Ferrarella
Top Secret Deliveries
Eve Walters's affair abruptly ended when she discovered her lover was
actually a drug dealer. Now, eight months later, she's pregnant with his
child when Adam Serrano walks back into her life—sending her into
labor! An undercover DEA agent, Adam is bound to protect Eve and their
child from the criminals he's trying to catch. But who will protect his heart
from falling for his new family?

#1581 THE CHRISTMAS STRANGER—Beth Cornelison
The Bancroft Brides
Trying to move forward with her life, widow Holly Bancroft Cole still
wants answers about her husband's murder. When she hires sexy but
secretive Matt Rankin to finish the renovations on her farmhouse for
Christmas, she never expects him to heal her heart. Except Matt is more
closely connected to Holly's past than either of them know—and once
revealed, it could destroy their second chance at love.

#1582 COLD CASE AFFAIR—Loreth Anne White
Wild Country
When pregnant Manhattan journalist Muirinn O'Donnell is forced to return
to her small Alaskan hometown, she slams right into the past she's tried so
hard to forget. Jett Rutledge doesn't want to see her either. They both have
secrets to keep, but as Muirinn investigates a twenty-year-old mystery,
danger sends her back into Jett's protective arms....

SRSCNMBPA0909